Evel Knievel Jumps
the Snake River Canyon

Also by Kelly Jones

Dana Pierson mystery series

Angel Boy

Bloodline and Wine

Lost and Found in Prague

Berkley/Random House titles

The Woman Who Heard Color

The Lost Madonna

The Seventh Unicorn

Evel Knievel Jumps the Snake River Canyon

new edition with stories from
those who were there

Kelly Jones

Ninth Avenue
PRESS

Ninth Avenue Press

Evel Knievel Jumps the Snake River Canyon was originally published by Ninth Avenue Press in 2014 as Evel Knievel Jumps the Snake River Canyon . . . and Other Stories Close to Home

Print ISBN   978-0-9914468-8-9

Cover Design by Ninth Avenue Press

Author Photo by Jim Jones

For Twin Falls family and friends, both old and new

Author's note

Evel Knievel Jumps the Snake River Canyon . . . and Other Stories Close to Home was originally published in 2014 to commemorate the 40th anniversary of Evel Knievel's launch over the Snake River Canyon in September 1974. It included a novella and several short stories set in small towns.

I was living in Boise at the time of Evel's jump, but I had returned to my hometown to bear witness. My own personal story of the event is as brief as the few seconds it took Evel to launch and then drop down toward the canyon floor. So, in preparing to write my fictitious account of the summer of Evel Knievel, I spoke to others who were living in Twin Falls at the time, mostly family members: an older brother who was serving in the Idaho National Guard and on call in case things got out of hand; a nineteen-year-old brother, off with his friends to watch the jump; a much younger brother, taking in the event from the small golf course at the Holiday Inn in a family group including me, our mom and dad, a sister, her husband, and a future brother-in-law.

Inspired by my youngest brother's recollections, I decided to tell my fictitious story from the point of view of a ten-year-old boy searching for a hero and something to make the prospect of spending the summer in the boring, hick town of Twin Falls more bearable. Pick's story remains as written for the 2014 publication in this second edition.

At the time I wrote the original story, there was talk of another stuntman or daredevil jumping the canyon in celebration of the 40th anniversary of Evel's launch, two teams competing to make it happen. As it turned out, this took much longer to accomplish. The X2 Skycycle, built to replicate Evel's original Skycycle, took off from the canyon rim over 42 years following Evel's performance, launching from the canyon's north side and landing on the south side, reversing the course of the original plan. It was done with far less fanfare. Evel had been gone for about nine years by then, having passed away in 2007. It wasn't a big deal without the one and only original Evel Knievel. No one could do it like Evel, though this Knievel-less jump in 2016 was dubbed a success.

While writing the original novella, I read several books on Evel Knievel and collected articles and newspaper stories from 1974 that I could use as resources. But, I discovered because Evel was often the source of these stories, and he was a promoter who at times tended to exaggerate, particularly when it came to crowd size and paychecks, I couldn't always rely on these numbers or even the specifics of events as initially reported.

So, for this second edition, I wanted to talk to real people who had been there. I set out to find my witnesses and move beyond the stories shared within my family. Several things became apparent as I talked to those willing to delve into their trove of memories. For one, these conversations were taking place anywhere from 48 to almost 50 years after the event, and memories can be a bit fuzzy, something all of my witnesses were willing to admit.

Yet, many of the recollections reported by those I interviewed were vivid, not so much in what they saw, but in what they had felt—when they witnessed the rough-looking strangers coming to town, the ill-fated launch, the crowds surging toward the canyon's rim, the vandalism on site, the vendors' booths, the food carts and trucks, the portable toilets and phones, destroyed.

As I talked to these witnesses, I found myself more interested in their stories than in the jump itself. Many were people whose families had been in Twin Falls since the early 1900s, and their roots were firmly planted in the Magic Valley soil. One had remained in Twin Falls, a number had moved to different parts of the State, two had relocated outside of Idaho.

I also found that people I had never spoken with before or even met were willing to share much of their own family histories. We talked about family connections, mutual friends and acquaintances, what our families did in Twin Falls, how they had contributed to what is now a community of over 50,000, more than double the population in 1974. Everyone seemed to be linked to the community in so many different ways. I found myself not only learning about their family stories but reliving much of mine, too.

I have many to thank, beginning with those who read the original novella published in 2014. For early readers, the late Coston Frederick, Judy Frederick, Franny Florence, Brian Florence, and Jim Jones, I owe you all a big debt of gratitude for sharing your thoughts and ideas. Thank you, also, to Mrezzie Putnam who read the revised edition.

For those who agreed to talk to me about their memories, Steve Swope, John Killen, David Whitehead, Charles Cosgriff, Rita Delaney, Jim Jones, and Sue Swenson Cummins, a big thank you. I told you all I would include a disclaimer—these are memories and not necessarily facts. So, dear readers, take these stories as you wish and please enjoy. I have attempted to write them as authentically as possible.

Table of Contents

EVEL KNIEVEL JUMPS THE SNAKE RIVER CANYON

I was ten years old the summer I came to live with Grandma Grace and Uncle Buddy in Twin Falls. It was 1974, the town's population hovered around 20,000, and the fingers of urban commerce had yet to stretch out to the canyon rim, digging into the lava rock, erecting big box stores selling electronics and shoes and books. The warehouses, stacked with groceries two dozen feet high, and the restaurants, touting breathtaking views of the Snake River Canyon while offering menu selections with names like tartare, ceviche, and prosciutto, had yet to be built.

Yet, it was this very canyon, almost 500 feet deep, 1,600 feet across, that would bring fame to the little town that summer.

Mom and I had driven over from Portland with only the vaguest plan, but somehow I knew she'd be leaving without me.

It was just the two of us, my dad having died fighting in the war in Viet Nam. I have no memory of him, though everyone says he looked a lot like my Uncle Michael.

Grandma Grace, a woman of fifty-something, with short cropped salt and pepper hair, possessed a let's-get-things-done attitude, and Uncle Buddy, according to Grandma, was content with getting nothing done at all. She harped on him constantly to get out and find a job or Uncle Sam would be knocking at his door. The draft had ended along with the U.S. involvement in the war that had taken my dad, so it was unlikely. I didn't know that at the time.

There were other things I didn't know—that a scandal called Watergate was winding down, that our President was on the verge of being impeached, that America, like my mom and me, and maybe Uncle Buddy, too, was in some kind of quandary as to where it was going.

These are the things I did know: my mom drank too much and she cried too much; we'd moved more times than I could count and I didn't have any friends; I was shorter than just about any other boy my age; the Idaho sun made my freckles pop out overnight (in Portland we'd had no more than a day of sunshine in the two and a half months we'd been there); my Grandma Grace was bossy and my Uncle Buddy, despite what Grandma Grace said, was just about the coolest person I'd ever known. He had dark hair like Elvis, pale blue eyes rimmed with long dark lashes, and rode a motorcycle that Grandma Grace said was going to kill him if the repossessor didn't come get it first. He bought it when he did have a job with a construction company, but he'd been fired for coming in late three days in a row, and I know for a fact that he was looking for a job because every day, after making us both a breakfast of bacon, eggs, toast, and often fried potatoes, he left to go look for work.

"This bacon is made right here in Twin Falls from those famous Falls Brand pigs," he always told me as he placed several pieces, nice and crisp the way I liked them, on my plate.

Everything in Twin Falls had some kind of reference to the falls, which was not really a twin falls at all. My mom took me down to the canyon and I was disappointed because it was barely one falls, let alone two.

But then we left the canyon and drove a few miles back down the road, into the canyon again along a winding road and she showed me something I figured she must have been saving up—the roaring Shoshone Falls.

"Now, what do you think of that?" she'd asked proudly as if she herself had something to do with this majestic scene.

"Totally cool," I replied. The falls rumbled, thundered like a wild beast as we stood with several others, tourists I guessed, on a concrete fenced-in pad overlooking the falls. Though it was a long ways down, I felt the cool spray across my face. It felt so good, sounded so good, the roar of the water, the sheer power, that I wanted to stand there all day, being with my mom, the water cooling me on that scorching Idaho day. I stared down at the rugged lava rock cliffs, noticing bits of trash, but also coins tossed out as if into a wishing well to make a wish. They'd caught on the rocky ledge, not made it down to the water, and I wondered if that meant those wishes would be denied.

I was tempted to ask for a coin to make a wish. She hadn't told me yet, but I sensed she'd be leaving soon, and I wanted to wish that she would stay or take me with her.

"Higher than Niagara Falls," she said and then, "You want to go for a burger and Coke?"

We didn't eat out much, even at the drive-in, so I knew this was a big treat, and I also guessed it was the last meal we'd share.

We drove back into town to the Arctic Circle, ordered burgers, fries with special sauce, and Cokes. We sat eating silently, both of us afraid to talk about what we knew was going to happen. Then she told me.

"I'm taking off tomorrow morning, early before you're up. I've had a job offer in Seattle, a friend of your dad's, a guy who served with him in Nam. His uncle works for a company that makes airplane parts and they need someone to help out in the office, and well . . ." She didn't cry, and neither did I, but we were both on the verge. I dipped a fry into the special sauce, which everybody knew was just ketchup and mayonnaise, though the drive-in wanted you to think it was some secret special recipe. I chewed on the fry and it tasted soggy and greasy, cold at that.

"When I'm settled, know for sure things will work out, get a place to live . . . For now Grandma Grace will take care of you." She smiled and I could tell the smile didn't come easy. "Uncle Buddy can help out too, at least until he has a job."

Somehow I was getting the feeling I came from a family of losers. Grandma Grace was the only one who had a real job, and the way Mom was talking it didn't sound like hers was a for-sure thing either.

The next morning, she was gone. When I woke, I glanced over at the twin bed, a nightstand away from mine, where my mother had been sleeping during the time she'd been here with me, and it was empty, made up tidily as if no one had even slept there last night. A shaft of light fell through the blinds, creating a pattern on the white bedspread that made me think of prison bars.

I could hear Grandma Grace call from the kitchen. "Better get out here, unless you want to eat a cold breakfast."

I lay for a while, then got up and slipped on my pajama bottoms, actually cut-off bottoms that Grandma Grace had sewed for me. I was used to sleeping in my underwear, but she'd made me these pajamas—tops and bottoms, with sailboats on them. When I told Mom they were too hot she asked Grandma to cut them off, which she did in about a minute and hemmed them up so I had shorty pajamas, which were pretty girlish if it hadn't been for the sailboats against a blue background. The matching pajama top lay folded neatly in the top drawer of the dresser.

When I went into the kitchen, wearing my white, slept-in T-shirt and my sailboat pajama bottoms—a nice compromise so as not to hurt my grandmother's feelings—Grandma Grace was getting ready to take off for her job at the J. C. Penney store downtown, where she worked in the fabric and notions department, and Uncle Buddy was finishing up his bacon and eggs, scraping the yolk off the plate with a piece of toast. Grandma Grace always ate early, a bowl of bran cereal that smelled so bad I was happy to have that bacon smell to cover it up. For the past few days I had stayed in bed, waiting to smell that bacon, hoping when I got up Grandma Grace would be gone.

"You're up," she said as I walked into the kitchen, wishing my mom was still there, yet knowing she was gone. The stern line of Grandma Grace's lips lifted in an almost smile as if she was happy to see me.

"I'm on my way out," she said. "Put some of that lotion on your face, ChapStick on your lips."

Instinctively, I reached up and ran my finger over my rough mouth. I hated that word *lips*, made me sound like a girl.

"It's in the second shelf in the bathroom," she went on. The constant sage-scented breeze blowing into town from the desert left my skin as dry as dust and my lips chapped and blistered like a sunburned baby. Mom and I had been used to the moist, rainy northwest and in this Idaho desert we were constantly dry. Mom had been reminding me to get *moisturized* as she called it, and I guess this job had fallen on Grandma Grace now.

Buddy, who sat drinking coffee, looked over at me and made this motion like he was a girl putting on lipstick. He made a smack, smack sound.

Nobody said anything about my mom, and I wondered if they just didn't want to talk about her deserting me. She'd explained she'd be gone when I got up and I was sure she'd told them too, though we hadn't talked about that. It dawned on me that morning that maybe they didn't even want me here.

"Ride your bike downtown about noon, Pick," Grandma

5

Grace said, "and we can have hamburgers over at Crowley's." She started down the hall toward her bedroom.

Two days in a row now, I thought, which put a new twist on this whole deal. Maybe everybody was feeling sorry for me and I'd get hamburgers and soda every day.

I stood for a moment, glancing around, and could hear Grandma Grace already coming back down the hall.

"Chore list for you on the counter," she said as she stood in the doorway, sticking her arms through her sweater, adjusting her purse from one hand to the other as she did. I knew it would be much too hot for a sweater as the day progressed. Old ladies always seemed to be cold around here, showing up for Sunday Mass with sweaters and jackets and all.

"On the counter," she repeated with a wave of her now-sweatered arm, as if I hadn't been listening. Then she turned back, her footsteps echoing through the hall. I heard the back door shut, then moments later the car revving up as the garage door jerked up, then slammed back down after she'd pulled out.

Buddy glanced over from the sink where he stood rinsing off his plate. "Left one for me too," he whispered. "A note. GET A JOB." His voice rose as if all the letters on his list were penned with caps.

I sat down at the table and Uncle Buddy slid a plate over in front of me with a flare and his usual offering of bacon, eggs, and toast. He poured me a glass of orange juice.

"Thanks," I said, picking up a fork.

A few days ago, before she left, I'd heard my mom and Grandma talking about Buddy not being a very good role model for a boy who was certainly in need of one. "He's got nothing but his dad," Grandma Grace said, "and, if you haven't noticed, the boy doesn't talk about his dad, maybe because he doesn't even remember him. A boy needs someone to relate to, someone who's there, and Buddy . . ."

"Buddy's doing his best right now, Mom. The breakup with Marcie was hard. He'll come around. Buddy always does. He's

6

suffering a broken heart right now."

"He needs a job, something to occupy his time, earn some money," Grandma Grace said without feeling. "Heaven knows he's not out there looking, unless he's looking in the bars . . ."

"Needs time," my mom said. "Sometimes it's easier when they're gone, but with Marcie—in a place the size of Twin, well, he's bound to run into her."

"He needs to make some money," Grandma had come back coldly.

I stabbed into my eggs as Buddy took a final swig of his coffee, and then rinsed off his cup and stuck it in the drainer, then tossed me a smile and a wave. So I sat alone, poking at the two fried eggs that had already started to jell. They were cold, the yolks staring up at me like two bright yellow eyes. The bacon was cold too, but was still the best thing I'd eaten here in Idaho, best bacon I'd ever eaten anywhere. I loaded some homemade strawberry jam on the toast, and then when I finished I got up and made another piece. On the counter, next to the toaster, I spotted a paper that must have been Grandma's list. I could see my name, PICK, spelled out in large letters that looked like it was written for a five-year-old. I didn't bother to read it. I heard the toilet in the half-bath in the hall flush, the back door slam, and then the roar of Buddy's motorcycle. Sitting alone, I finished my breakfast, forcing down one of the eggs, dumping the other in the trash. I squirted some dish soap into the sink, ran hot water, scrubbed off my plate, rinsed, dried it, and put it back in the cupboard, then guzzled the rest of my orange juice, rinsed off my glass and put it away. Then I grabbed the note and read.

Clean up dishes was the first thing on the list, and I'd already done that. I wondered if I was supposed to do Buddy's too. He'd rinsed off his plate and coffee cup, put them in the drainer, but hadn't bothered to use any dish soap, or dry them off. I slipped them back into the sink, still filled with soapy water, cleaned them up, rinsed, then took the dishtowel, swiped it over the cup, then the plate, and put them away, then hung the towel on the bar under the sink.

The second item on the list: *make your bed*, then, *put dirty clothes in hamper, gather and take out the garbage. (Be sure to gather all trash: kitchen, baths, my bedroom, Uncle Buddy's, yours.) Get it out no later than 10:00. Garbageman comes between 10 and noon.*

Grandma Grace was one of these organized people, so different from my mom and Uncle Buddy. I wondered about my Grandpa Jack, who I barely remembered. I don't think he was the organized type either, and wondered if people were just made the way they were made from the beginning, if Grandma Grace's lists and sense of organization were something she was born with. Though I always thought things through, I didn't know yet if I was the list-making type like my grandma.

I went into my bedroom, which was really my mother's bedroom when she was growing up. The twin beds were covered with soft, white bedspreads, cute girl pillows in purples and pinks, which—when the beds were made, like my mom's was now—were thrown over the bed pillows that were rolled neatly then covered with the upper part of the bedspread. The dresser was also white, the curtains a frilly fabric with a pattern of butterflies in the colors and fabric of the pillows. My mom had added a few posters on the wall—bands popular when she was a teen—but I'd never heard of any of them. Somehow all this femininity stood as confirmation that this was temporary, that I wouldn't be here long. Though Mom's bed was made, I wondered again if she'd even slept in it, if she'd left right after she'd come in to tell me good night. I hadn't heard her come back in, or leave, and the fact that I'd slept so soundly when I knew she was leaving seemed a betrayal of sorts.

I made the bed, picked up the dirty jeans I'd thrown on the floor, my socks, and underwear and took them and threw them into the hamper in the laundry room. I wondered if eventually I'd be promoted to doing the laundry. I knew Grandma Grace was picky about that, and I didn't imagine she'd trust me to do it right.

8

I found a medium-size garbage bag in a box under the kitchen sink and started through the rooms gathering up the trash. I did the bathrooms first, then my mom's room, finding a couple of tissues with her lipstick on them, but that was all, as if that's all she'd left me.

Buddy's room was a big mess with books and magazines piled high, clothes strewn about the floor, an empty peanut can on the nightstand, a Butterfinger candy bar wrapper peeking out from under the bed. I looked at the books on the nightstand, reading the spines. Hemingway. Steinbeck. Faulkner. I wondered if I should gather up all this strewn garbage or just take what was in the trash can, which wasn't much other than a few gum wrappers. A couple of beer cans sat on the window ledge. Grandma Grace hated smoking, forbid it in the house, but I could tell from the smell of Buddy's room that he was smoking in here, and I guessed those beer cans were filled with old cigarette butts. I'd never seen Buddy smoke unless he was drinking beer. I'd seen him using one of those cans as an ashtray out on the back patio a few days earlier, before my mom left. They were both drinking beer, talking in hushed voices that all but silenced when I went out to join them.

I dumped the gum wrappers in the garbage bag and left Buddy's room, went down the hall to Grandma Grace's room. Neat as a pin, other than a pile of fabric stacked on her sewing machine. Another stack of patterns from her store. I walked over and noticed an especially bright fabric, all blues and reds and yellows, amidst the pastel floral prints Grandma Grace favored for her own blouses and summer dresses. Darned if that overly bright fabric wasn't filled with baseballs, footballs, and soccer balls. Was she planning on sewing me another pair of pajamas? I stared at the fabric for several moments, then slowly, carefully I unfolded it and looked it over. A repeating pattern of balls from every sport imaginable, but in unrealistic colors. Blue footballs, white and green soccer balls, yellow baseballs. I glanced over at the mini chest where I knew she kept her needles and spools of thread. And sewing scissors. I opened the top drawer and didn't even have to rummage around to find the scissors. I slid my fingers into the two oval openings, surprised at how heavy it felt in my hand. Then, carefully, I started to snip, doubling the fabric over in the middle, cutting a big jagged square out of the center. Meticulously I refolded it, hiding the cutout, wondering if Grandma Grace really thought this was masculine, that a ten-year-old kid like me, a boy who'd never played a single sport in his life, would like it. I took the square of fabric and dumped it in the trash bag I'd been carrying around from room to room, and then I trudged back into the kitchen and added the egg shells and plastic bacon wrappers from that morning, along with several days of carrot peels, soggy lettuce and tomato tops.

I tied a knot in the top of the plastic bag and lugged it out the back door, not even bothering to put on my shoes, opened the gate out of the yard to the alley and lifted the metal lid off the old trash can that looked like it had been in the family for at least half a century. A strong whiff of leftover rotting trash jumped out at me, so I tossed the large trash bag in quick as I could and replaced the lid. A few pieces of dried-up paper towel, maybe from earlier in the week, stuck to the outside of the trash can, so I pried them loose, lifted the lid a tad and poked them inside. Just as I replaced the lid a second time, WHACK.

Something hard had hit me in the head. I reached back and felt a wet patch on my scalp. I looked at my finger—blood—and realized someone had hit me with a rock. Quickly I reached down, grabbed a handful of stones and pebbles from the alley, feeling some gritty dirt tagging along, and positioned myself behind the large metal trash can. Another rock flew from across the alley, missing me by inches.

I could see a head peeking out from behind a trash can on the other side of the alley a couple of houses down, then another head.

"What the heck are you doing?" I yelled.

"What are you doing in our alley?" the biggest head yelled back as he lobbed another rock across the alley. It hit the trash can with a metallic ping.

"You're a lousy shot," I hollered.

The little head was bobbing out to get a look, then back for protection, though I had yet to throw a single rock.

"This isn't your alley," I snarled.

"Is so," the big head yelled.

"Public alley," I came back. "That city garbage truck will be barreling down this morning picking up trash—"

"You're the trash," the little head hollered and laughed. So did his big brother. They had to be brothers, I realized. They had identical flattop haircuts and piggy-looking upturned noses.

"You look like a couple of pigs," I yelled, throwing my words across the alley as if they were rocks, attempting to sharpen the edges to be as hurtful as possible. "Wallowing around in the trash. Maybe this is your alley. Piggy trash alley."

In my head, I heard my mom's voice, "Sticks and stones may break your bones, but words can never—"

"Danny," a woman's voice called. "Ricky." She made her way through the back yard toward the alley, pocketbook in one hand, car keys dangling from the other. She stopped as she approached the two boys using the trash can as cover. Obviously their mother, as she had the same upturned nose.

"What's going . . ." She glanced over toward me. "Hi," she said cautiously, then, "You must be Grace's grandson." Her voice was sweet and for a moment I thought she might come over and shake my hand. I cowered behind the trash can, having just realized I was still barefooted, wearing my shorty pajama cutoff bottoms with the sailboats, hoping the two boys hadn't got a look at them before I jumped for cover.

"I heard you were coming to visit this summer," the mother said. "We've been out of town this past week and a half. Not sure Grace told me . . . what's your name?"

"Pick," I said, without thinking. It wasn't really my name, but

11

it was what everyone called me. My real name's Michael. Michael Andrew Patterson. When I was a baby my Uncle Michael, my dad's brother, had called me Pickle, I think maybe because it sounded sort of like Michael, and he figured he was already Michael and we needed another name for me. Somehow it stuck and had eventually been shortened to Pick. I'd heard all the jokes—*like, that mean you pick your nose, and eat your boogers?* Or, if I told them it was short for Pickle, *is your weenie a green pickle?* I was sure that Ricky would be saying something now if his sweet Momma hadn't been standing right there. In my head, I was kicking myself for being so stupid. Nobody knew me here and I could make up a new name. I should have said my name was Mike.

"Well, welcome to the neighborhood, Pick," Ricky and Danny's mom said, "I'm Mrs. Edsen and you've met the boys. You'll have to come over some time and play. We're in a bit of a rush this morning," she said tucking her pocketbook under her arm.

The two boys were standing now, not crouching like a couple cowards behind the trash can. The older stood, feet spread, hands on his hips. The younger, who I guessed to be about six or seven, nuzzled up to his mother. I noticed they were both wearing swimming trunks, the little boy now digging around trying to rearrange his privates.

"Well, boys, let's go." She turned, then glanced back at me over her shoulder. "We're headed off to swimming lessons. You like to swim?"

I stood now, still behind the trash can, fist still clutching the rocks. I nodded, though I really wasn't much of a swimmer. But every kid likes to swim.

"Maybe you and the boys can go over to Harmon Park one of these afternoons." As if we were best buddies, as if her kids hadn't just split my head open with an alley rock. I reached back with my clean hand, the one that wasn't filled with alley rocks and dirt, and discovered it had already stopped bleeding.

"It's closed for lessons every morning," Mrs. Edsen added, as if she'd given this more thought, "but opens in the afternoon for everyone. How about you going over with the boys sometime?"

She didn't wait for my answer, but I thought maybe I'd ask Buddy or Grandma Grace about swimming at Harmon Park. With my mom gone and no friends, I needed something to do.

I puttered around the rest of the morning, watched a bit of TV. There was nothing good, just soap operas, and they only got one channel. Just before noon I changed into my jeans and buttoned cotton shirt, went out to the storage shed attached to the garage and hopped on my bike, which stood next to my mom's. The bike I'd been riding since I got to Twin Falls was really an old bike Buddy had years ago. He'd fixed it up with new tires and a new seat. I rode the six blocks to downtown, passing the library and City Park with its tiny, round wading pool, which actually looked pretty good since the air was starting to warm. I wished I would have remembered to put on that ChapStick because I could already feel my lips splitting and cracking. When I got downtown I leaned the bike up against the J. C. Penney store and went in and over to the fabric section. I didn't see Grandma Grace, so I asked the lady at the cash register.

"Oh, you must be Pick," she said, reminding me that this would have to be my name here in Twin Falls. I'd change it to Mike when I went to live with my mom in Seattle. This was such a stupid town anyway. Full of a bunch of hicks, I thought, and had to laugh as a cluster of nonsense words made a rhyme in my head. Hicks. Pricks. Dicks. The realization that my name, Pick, was a good rhyme, too, slipped right in, lining up with all those words, reminding me why people always made fun of me.

Just then Grandma Grace came out of the back room, her purse swung over her shoulder. "We're headed to Crowley's to grab some burgers," she told the lady at the register, who smiled as if we were off on a great adventure. "Might take a little extra time today."

I left my bike at the store and we walked the half block down to Crowley's. It was really a drugstore with a soda fountain bar in the back, and in all honesty they did have great burgers. We'd already ridden our bikes down once to have lunch with Grandma Grace when Mom was here. The burgers were twice the size of those from the Arctic Circle, and the fries were hand cut, made—according to the little ditty running across the menu—from real Idaho potatoes.

"Hi there, Grace," the woman behind the counter greeted us as we sat down on the round swivel stools at the counter.

"Afternoon, Marcene. This is my grandson, Pick," she introduced me. "Pick, this is Mrs. Hacking."

"Visiting your grandma this summer?" she asked with a smile.

"Just visiting, yep," I said.

We put in our order. I asked Grandma Grace if I could get a chocolate milkshake and she said sure. We sat and watched as Mrs. Hacking poured in the ingredients: milk, vanilla ice cream, chocolate syrup, and spun it around in the noisy milkshake maker.

A couple of men in business suits and ties came in and sat at the other end of the bar.

"Six million dollars, that's what he's getting," one of them said. "Can you believe that?" He shook his head in disbelief. "And that's just the upfront money. Arum says they'll be pulling in more than that when it's all said and done."

"Could be a real financial boon for the community," the other said as he picked up a menu. "Got any of that chicken salad today, Marcene?"

"Just whipped some up. How about you?" she said, shooting a grin toward the other businessman. "Take your regular cheeseburger today?"

"You got it, Marcene," he replied, then turned to his companion. "It's sure going to put us on the map. I hear they paid Tim Qualls $35,000 just to lease the land."

Another man, this one in an open-collar shirt and a shiny

14

forehead, walked up to the counter. "Could bring in a bunch of riffraff, too," he said, sliding into the conversation as easily as he slid onto the barstool. "They plan on selling 200,000 tickets."

"That's a joke," one of the men said. "That'd increase the city population by a good ten times for the weekend. Not going to happen."

"Might have to prepare for it. Sheriff Corder's talking about pulling in the State Police," one of them added with concern.

"National Guard's more likely," the third man chimed in.

I could see Grandma Grace shaking her head, but she didn't join in the conversation. "Get your chores done?" she asked me.

"Yep," I said.

"Good." She gave me a pat on the head. I flinched when she touched the spot where I'd been hit by the alley rock.

"What's wrong with your head?"

"Bumped it on the kitchen cupboard when I was cleaning up," I lied.

Her eyes narrowed for a moment and then she said, "Maybe we could set you up on an allowance."

"I don't plan on staying long, so don't set me up on a salary or anything," I came back and she emitted a little laugh out of the corner of her mouth.

Mrs. Hacking poured our milkshakes out of the big stainless steel milkshake maker into two tall fancy glasses, spooned on a bit of whipped cream, put a cherry on top of each, jabbed in a straw and spoon, set one in front of me and the other in front of Grandma Grace.

The straws stood stiff as smokestacks, and I could see right away the shakes were too thick to slurp through a tiny hole. I popped the cherry in my mouth, discarded the stem in the ashtray, then chased the sweetness down with an enormous spoonful of milkshake. The cold, smooth texture felt good as it passed over my dry mouth, and the whipped cream and chocolate tasted like magic as they touched my tongue and slid down my throat.

"Did you see that footage on Wide World of Sports?" one of the businessmen said. "The fella's an idiot. Broken every bone in his body, as I hear. Was in a coma for a month after that jump at Caesars."

"With a pocketful of money," his friend added.

"I hear he has his own bank vault in Butte," the newcomer joined in. "Walks around with a gold-encrusted, diamond-studded cane."

"Well, let's stuff some of that money in our pockets, too," the first one said.

All three of the men laughed as Mrs. Hacking delivered our fries and cheeseburgers.

"Do you know about Harmon Park?" I asked Grandma Grace. I removed the onion and tomato from my burger and shoved them over to the edge of my plate. I kept the lettuce, rearranged the pickles, grabbed the bright yellow plastic bottle on the counter and squirted some mustard on my patty in a pattern of concentric circles. "I hear they have a swimming pool." I slapped the top bun back on and took an enormous bite.

She nodded, but I could see in her eyes she was wondering where this came from. "Buddy tell you he'd take you over there to the pool?"

I swallowed before answering, remembering Grandma Grace's admonition about talking with your mouth full. "I heard some kids in the alley when I took out the trash."

"The Edsen kids? Ricky and Danny?"

"Yeah, I think so."

"You meeting some friends?"

Friends wouldn't pelt you with rocks, I thought, but instead I asked, "Think I might go swimming?"

"Well, now," Grandma Grace said thoughtfully, "if you keep doing your chores, I think we could work something out."

I squirted a glob of ketchup on my plate, then a pile of mayo, stirring them around with a fry, mixing my own special sauce.

"I've been looking for something at the store," Grandma

Grace said, "a nice fabric to make some new curtains. Those hanging in your mom's room are pretty old. I picked something out, but then got thinking maybe you'd like to do that yourself. Choose a nice fabric."

I'd just stuffed a special-sauced fry in my mouth and now it felt like a lump of concrete. Was that fabric I'd mutilated in her bedroom for curtains, not pajamas? There was surely enough for curtains, more than enough. I swallowed hard. Either way—pajamas or curtains—I didn't like it, but I could feel some guilt filling a space inside me right next to the burger and fries.

I swallowed again. "Yeah, that'd be nice," I said.

After we finished, we walked back to J. C. Penney, and Grandma Grace asked if I'd come in and look over some of the fabrics. I picked out a plain blue and brown stripe, with a little bit of white, and she laughed and said she guessed she didn't know much about ten-year-old boys, that she'd originally chosen something completely different, but she figured she could use it for making her quilts. I knew she sewed up some quilts to take out to the pediatric department at the hospital, and she'd asked me to go with her one of these days soon. We picked out some kids' quilt fabrics too, cute teddy bears for the little kids, some fluffy girlie stuff with flowers and ribbons, and some of those boys' trucks and sports, which Grandma Grace was maybe finally figuring out I didn't like and was too old for anyway.

Grandma said she had to go back to work and asked me what I was going to do for the rest of the day and I said maybe I'd just watch TV. She suggested I stop at the library on my way home and get some books, but I told her I didn't have a card. She didn't say anything, but I could see she was thinking maybe I needed to get one, that I was going to be pretty bored watching one channel on TV all day.

I hopped on my bike and started back. A bunch of kids splashed around in the wading pool at City Park and I stopped to watch. The midday sun was beating down now and I was tempted to take off my shoes and dip them into that mini pool, but it was just little kids, nobody over five at the most, and the deepest part probably wouldn't even reach up to my knees. It was so shallow they were crawling around, growling at each other like they were fierce, wild animals.

"No, I'm the alligator," one kid shouted to a smaller child.

I noticed a girl, maybe a couple of years older than me, sitting on the edge of the seat of a nearby picnic table reading a book. She had long blonde hair that she kept pushing back off her face and tucking behind her ear. She looked up and over toward the wading pool every time she turned a page, and I thought maybe she was a babysitter or something. A couple of the kids seemed to be quarreling, and she got up and walked over and bent down, talking to them, breaking up the fight. I couldn't hear her words, but, from the way she tilted her head and smiled, I could see she was doing this in a gentle, caring way. When she stood and turned to go back to her reading, she caught my eye and I noticed, seeing her from the front, how pretty she was and that she was probably at least fourteen. The way she looked at me, I could tell she thought I was staring at her, which I guess I was. I dropped my gaze, hopped on my bike and headed back to the house.

I was wishing Buddy would be home. I wondered what he was doing all day, if he was really looking for a job. I jumped off my bike and walked it back through the side gate, heading toward the shed next to the garage. I could hear some shouting coming from the alley. I dropped my bike in the grass and went over to the fence to see what all the commotion was about.

"No, I'm going to jump first," Ricky shouted at Danny, using a mean big brother voice.

"You always get to do everything first," Danny screamed. They were on their bikes, those low stingray type bikes with the high curved handlebars and banana seats that made my bike look like leftover trash. Danny was actually just standing next to his, tight grip on those handlebars. I got the impression that he couldn't keep his balance and shout that loud at the same time.

18

Ricky took off, popped a wheelie, spraying up some dust and rocks, and then let out a big yahoo. He glanced over at me before I could dodge for cover. He didn't say anything and neither did I. I turned and started to walk back to get my bike and put it away, but by then he'd pedaled over to the fence.

"Got a bike?" he yelled and I turned. He'd stopped riding, still sitting on his bike, feet on the ground. He folded his thick, pudgy arms over his chest.

"Nothing fancy," I replied, eyeing his bike that looked pretty new. "Just an old bike my Uncle Buddy fixed up for me."

"Buddy, he rides a motorcycle," he said with a head toss. It would have been a toss of his hair, if he'd had any hair. "He's cool," he added, even as I thought how uncool that flattop haircut was.

"Yeah," I said, then, "How come you're riding in the alley? Isn't it kind of rocky and bumpy? How come you're not riding in the street?"

"We're playing Evel Knievel," he answered as if this might explain everything.

I didn't say anything and I know I must have had a confused look on my face because he said, "You don't even know who Evel Knievel is? Do you?" His voice had a you're-dumb-as-dirt tone to it.

"Yeah," I said. Everyone knew who Evel Knievel was, but the way he said it, I thought he was trying to trick me or make me say something stupid. "Yeah, he—"

"Jumps snakes and wild animals and cars and busses and canyons on his motorcycle. He was going to jump over the Grand Canyon, but the government wouldn't let him. So, now he's going to jump over the Snake River Canyon," he explained with a wide sweep of his arm in the direction of the canyon.

When I didn't reply with the expected *I'm not stupid, I know that*, he said, "So where have you been that you don't even know about Evel Knievel jumping the Snake River Canyon?"

In Portland, I thought about saying, a much bigger place than this, but somehow I did feel stupid, like I had no idea about anything, and this kid from this hick town was telling me all about what was going on in the world, the biggest news obviously being that Evel Knievel was jumping the Snake River Canyon.

"So, what are *you* jumping?" I finally came back. "Snakes or wild animals? Bet this alley's full of them." I glanced out toward the alley, then at his brother, who was now picking his nose. "Or wild pigs? Nose-picking pigs." Danny's finger immediately dislodged itself from his nose, and he stuck it in his pocket as if hiding the boogers he'd just dug out.

"Garbage cans," Ricky said and folded his arms close to his chest again. "Waiting for my friend Jeff." His little brother had abandoned his bike, just dumped it right there in the alley, and was now hanging on Grandma's fence, his feet on the lower rung, his chin precariously placed between two points of the slats. "We got a ramp, too," Ricky said, and then motioning toward his brother, he told me, "He's not strong enough to help, not smart enough, or got good balance to jump."

"Am too," Danny snarled.

"Want to help?" Ricky almost sounded like he meant it. "Ramp's in the garage."

I shrugged. "Nothing better to do, I guess," I said nonchalantly.

He motioned with his head for me to follow as he took off on his bike. I stood for a moment considering, then crossed the alley following him as Danny tagged along, walking his bike.

The ramp, I could see, really wasn't a ramp at all, but a bunch of old discarded two-by-fours and scraps of plywood. I could also see someone (Ricky and, I assumed, his friend Jeff, who had yet to show up), had been sawing away on a piece of plywood, I think to make the surface of the ramp.

As Ricky sawed I sat on the concrete floor of the garage, watching, waiting for him to give me a job. The garage was full of boxes and barrels and shelves, but there wasn't enough room for a car, and I guessed they parked it out on the street like a bunch of the neighbors.

"So, how long you going to be at your grandma's?" Ricky asked after a while.

"Not long," I said, not committing to either a lengthy stay or this possible friendship.

"How old are you?"

"Ten."

"Yeah, me too." He glanced up from his plywood and grinned.

"I'm six," Danny said. He'd been wandering around the garage, not really helping, just looking through a bunch of boxes and coffee cans, pulling out a nut or bolt here or there, placing them on a work bench built into the garage wall.

"Why don't you put those boards together?" Ricky said, motioning to a pile of cut up two-by-fours that had been placed on the floor like a puzzle. I guessed from the configuration, that these were the supports that would prop up the ramp for the proper angle. He handed me a hammer and a tin can filled with nails.

It felt awkward at first, but I got the hang of it without Ricky making some mean comment or asking if I'd ever done this before, which in truth I hadn't. We worked away, Ricky sawing, me hammering with a rhythm that provided a strange and unexplainable comfort. We didn't talk much, and by now Danny had wandered back to the house.

We lugged the pieces of our ramp out into the alley and set it up. It wasn't really level, the supports not even or matched. I knew nothing about ramps, but I could see this wasn't a good one and likely wouldn't hold up if anyone actually tried to use it to jump anything. It sat at a precarious angle, and I envisioned it flying apart as soon as a bike wheel touched the surface. I thought Ricky would blame me for the lopsidedness, but he didn't. He'd helped with the second support, and it didn't even look as good as the one I'd put together. We started rolling out some of the garbage cans lined up along the alley, one or two at each residence. I knew there was something wrong here; these weren't really ours, other than the one from his house and my grandma's. But nobody came out to make us stop, and Ricky explained this was the only day of the week this would work. After the garbageman came, they were all empty. After that, no luck, because people started filling them up again. I wondered why he didn't think of something else to jump or somewhere else.

We started out with five garbage cans, but both of us could see that was too many. So we rolled two back to their proper places in the alley and lined up three, top side up, lids on. There was no way that ramp was big enough, or long enough, or steep enough, and even if we could clear three upright garbage cans, it was pretty obvious we'd need an additional ramp of equal height and angle on the other side for a smooth landing.

"Maybe we should set the cans on their sides," I suggested, using my most cooperative, unaccusing voice. I knew this was never going to work, but didn't want to say it out loud. Ricky thought for a moment, hand rubbing his chin. Without answering, he started pushing cans over on their sides, creating a terrible racket and rattle, stirring up dust. I was surprised some grownup didn't come running and hollering out one of the back doors.

When we finally got the cans arranged, it didn't look nearly as impressive, although it reduced the height considerably.

We realigned the ramp, and Ricky hopped on his bike. He took a couple of runs along the side of the ramp-garbage-can setup as if he were studying the angles and distances. I could see he wasn't too excited about trying it, and for a moment I thought he was going to offer the first jump to me, and I wasn't too thrilled about that possibility. Even if we cleared those cans, even if that slapped-together ramp—and despite our effort that's exactly what it was—held up, that would be a tough landing. With the alley filled with rocks, I could only envision

22

the scrapes and cuts. And blood.

"We might think some more about the landing," I said slowly, cautiously.

He laughed. "Back to the drawing board," he said, which actually made sense to me. What we needed was a plan, a real plan. Just hammering some boards together, then lining up a bunch of garbage cans was pretty darn stupid, if not dangerous.

"Help me," he said impatiently, and I could see he intended to carry the ramp pieces back into the garage.

"What about the garbage cans?"

"Yeah," he replied, shoulders stooped. "Why don't you take them back and I'll drag the boards,"—he wasn't calling it a ramp anymore—"back to my garage."

Just then, I heard his mom calling from the backyard. "Ricky, time for dinner."

"Got to go," he said. "Maybe see you tomorrow?" he asked hopefully.

"Yeah, okay," I said, feeling a smile tugging at my mouth. I helped him with the boards, and then said I'd take care of the garbage cans since I didn't want him getting into trouble with his mom. When he was gone, I started to drag two of the garbage cans down the alley. I placed one at Ricky's house, another at his neighbors', and then I retrieved the one that belonged to Grandma Grace.

By the time I'd returned the garbage cans to their proper places in the alley and put my bike, that I'd left out in the yard all afternoon, back in the shed, Grandma Grace was pulling into the garage. Buddy still wasn't home, the spot where he parked his motorcycle in the shed empty.

"Here," she said in a weary voice, "help me with these grocery bags."

I grabbed a couple of bags and followed her into the house. She carried a package from her store that I guessed probably contained the fabric for my curtains, as well as the stuff I'd helped pick out for the hospital quilts.

"What did you do this afternoon?" she asked.

"Me and Ricky Edsen were riding bikes." Another lie, though pretty close to the truth. I knew she wouldn't like it if I told her what we'd really been doing. I also knew that I'd go back to the alley tomorrow.

When we got inside, Grandma Grace asked if Buddy's motorcycle was in the shed, and I told her no, that I hadn't seen him all afternoon. She put the package from her store in her bedroom, then unloaded the grocery bags and started dinner.

The pork chops were sizzling when we heard Buddy's motorcycle zipping up the alley, then pulling into the shed.

When he opened the back door and strutted in, he had a big grin on his face and smelled of beer.

Grandma Grace shot him a glance of disapproval but she didn't say anything.

"Got a job," he said, sitting down at the kitchen table, slapping it and causing the plates, glasses and silverware I was setting up to do a little dance. "Just for the rest of the summer, but it pays pretty good, and maybe I can make enough to go back up to U of I, back to school this fall."

I knew Buddy had gone to college up north at the University for a couple of years, but then he'd run out of money, come back home to work, then lost his job at the construction company for coming in late three days in a row. Though Grandma made a big deal out of his not working or going to school, my mom always said he was really smart and if he found the right thing he'd be okay.

"Just for the summer?" Grandma Grace asked, digging for more information before expressing disapproval. Or possibly approval.

"Until September."

"Doing what?"

"Bodyguard," he said and grinned. "For none other than the famous daredevil and impresario Evel Knievel."

Grandma Grace's eyes grew as wide as that serving platter

24

she was slapping the pork chops onto. She didn't say anything for several moments as she finished making the gravy, other than, "Applesauce on the table, Pick," as she motioned toward the fridge.

"Will you say grace?" she asked me as we sat.

After I said the prayer and we passed around the applesauce, potatoes, gravy, peas, and pork chops, Grandma Grace said, "Well, at least that should work until September when he kills himself. School will be starting up about then."

That night I barely slept I was so excited. We'd stayed up late talking about what was happening in Twin Falls that summer, then in bed I'd strained to hear more as Grandma Grace and Buddy kept up the chatter. I understood now that the men downtown were talking about Evel Knievel, and he really was going to jump the Snake River Canyon for six million dollars. Buddy had told me and Grandma Grace that they'd set the date for Sunday, September 8, at 2:30 in the afternoon.

Grandma Grace said, "Well, you'd think he could pick a day other than Sunday when everybody'd be going to church, but, then, maybe he'll need all those prayers, because he has no chance in hell,"—she actually used the word hell—"of making it over that canyon on a motorcycle."

The jump was scheduled for just a little over two months away, but, according to Buddy, Evel had been leasing the land on the south side of the canyon for a couple of years now, though nothing much had been done to prepare for a real jump. Now in a whirlwind of activity, they were finishing up the launch ramp, getting a flying motorcycle built, and starting a cross-country tour after the Fourth of July holiday to tell the rest of the world about September 8, in Twin Falls, Idaho.

"Maybe I can get you an autograph," Buddy told me as we ate breakfast the next morning. "Or maybe one of those Evel Knievel toy stunt cycles. You don't have one of those, do you?"

Buddy stuffed a spoonful of eggs in his mouth, followed by an enormous gulp of milk.

The Evel Knievel toy stunt cycle had been the most popular toy the previous Christmas. It could turn and spin and run up the wall, probably jump a canyon too. It was like a crazy, flying motorcycle, like Evel Knievel would use to jump over the Snake River Canyon. So many kids had wanted one of those stunt cycles that the toy company that made them ran out. At least that's what my mom told me. I knew she couldn't afford one anyway.

I couldn't wait to tell Ricky that Buddy was going to be a bodyguard for Evel Knievel. After breakfast, after Buddy took off, I hurried out the back door, ran through the alley, and knocked on his back door. His mother answered.

"Oh, hi, Pick. The boys are fishing with their dad. Won't be back 'til Sunday night." She gazed down at me with a sympathetic smile that seemed to say, I know you don't have a dad, and I know the only time you've ever been fishing was when your Uncle Michael took you three years ago.

"Oh, okay," I said, attempting to keep the disappointment out of my voice.

"Why don't you ask if you can go swimming Monday afternoon," Mrs. Edsen said. "Pool opens at one. You and Ricky could ride your bikes over. I'm taking Danny to the doctor at two, but maybe I could bring him over later."

I smiled and nodded and bounded back through the alley. Buddy had already left for his new job. It was Grandma Grace's day off and I could hear her sewing machine humming away in the bedroom. I went in and saw that she'd already started in on the new curtains.

I sat down on the bed and told her about Mrs. Edsen's invitation to go swimming and she said that would be okay.

"How's he going to be bodyguarding a body if it's not even here?" I asked after sitting quietly for a while, listening to the steady, even rhythm of her sewing machine.

26

"What do you mean?"

"Buddy said Evel Knievel was going on a promotional tour all over the country. So if he's going to be somewhere else, how can Buddy be guarding him here?"

"Well," she said with a hint of exasperation in her voice, "I think that's a bit of a false title."

"What do you mean?"

"Buddy's working for Evel Knievel. But I think for right now he's just guarding the site, the place where they're going to launch on the south side of the canyon. Got to make sure to keep people out. All those curious eyes. All those blabbering mouths. When they're planning on charging admission for the actual jump, don't think they want a bunch of freeloaders getting an early look. Like Buddy said, they're doing some test launches. Big secret—they don't want the public knowing." She said these words real slow and low, like it was some kind of forbidden information, like there was actually someone else in the house that might hear. "If those tests go good, nobody'll pay. If they go bad . . . well."

"Like if they go bad it means he'll get killed?"

"That's what half the people are probably paying for anyway. To see a man killed."

"Or maybe if the tests go bad, he'll chicken out?" I asked.

"If he has any sense, which I'm not sure he does." She took the fabric off the machine, snipped a loose thread. "What do you think?" she asked, standing, holding up the curtains.

"Nice," I said, but what I really wanted was to hear more about Evel Knievel. "The businessmen down at Crowley's?" I asked. "They were all talking about Evel Knievel, weren't they?"

"Everyone wants a piece of the action. Everybody thinks there's money to be made. Several of the downtown merchants, restaurant people, well, they figure those people have to eat. And the hotel people. Of course, I imagine some of those tourists will be camping out. Tim Qualls is setting up a campsite by the launch, I hear. Heaven forbid, they'll be invading the city parks.

Numbers are going around like 200,000 coming in from out of town for the jump. Got to eat." She shook her head. "Got to poop, too," she added with a snicker. "Aren't enough Porta Potties in the entire county to take care of all that many people. We'll be importing potties! Either that or they'll all be pooping out there on Qualls' farm, just like a herd of cattle."

She pointed toward the chair next to her bed where she'd thrown the old curtains from my mom's room, then got up and showed me the hardware pinned along the top, about a dozen sharp metal pieces with hooks that looked like something between a giant paperclip and a super big safety pin. She showed me how to take them off and hook them onto the new curtains.

I sat on the bed working as Grandma Grace sewed up the other curtain. I've never seen anyone work a machine with such skill as Grandma Grace worked that sewing machine, twisting and pulling the fabric through while that needle bobbed up and down, slow at first, then fast as a jack hammer, then clipping and knotting. In no time at all she had the other curtain sewn up and ready to go. She helped me finish up the metal hardware hooks and then asked me to go into the laundry room and get the stepstool.

We went into my bedroom. I held the bulky fabric while she climbed on the stool, then I lifted the end, holding the rest like I was in a royal procession, raising up the back of a king's long cape while Grandma Grace started to attach the first curtain to the built-in hardware along the window frame.

"How can he jump across the canyon on a motorcycle?" I asked. "That's impossible, isn't it?"

"Don't believe it's really a motorcycle," she replied, stretching to secure the curtain hook. "Buddy said they started out with something with wheels to fool people into thinking it's a motorcycle, but sounds to me like it's really going to be some kind of rocket."

"So, what's the big deal about that?" I asked, confused. "They sent a man to the moon in a rocket."

Grandma Grace snorted as she stepped down, still holding a portion of the unattached fabric, moved the stool, climbed up again and went back to work. I moved along with her.

"I think the man is well . . ." She hesitated. "He's a bit full of the bull." She stepped off the stool, tested the pull cord as the curtains clicked open, then shut, slowly at first, then again with a quicker motion, open, then shut again. Then open. There were slatted blinds under the curtains, and I always figured the fabric curtains were just for show anyway.

"But he's certainly convinced a lot of people," Grandma Grace went on, "that this is some great feat." She glanced over at one twin bed, then the other, eyeing, I could see, those pretty pink and purple pillows. "A show, the man's just putting on a show, a huckster, at the best." She picked up one of the pillows and then another, stuffed them under her arm. "Maybe we could do some new pillows too. Find some fabrics matching the blue and brown stripes in the curtains. Maybe even dye the white chenille brown, so it all looks like it goes together. What do you think?"

I nodded a yes.

We made cheese and bologna sandwiches for lunch with home-canned peaches for dessert, then Grandma Grace said she was going over to the library and asked me if I wanted to go with her. Since there was nothing else to do I said okay.

She went back to the bedroom to get her purse and we walked the few blocks to the library. At the library Grandma Grace helped me sign up for a card and then sent me downstairs to the children's library. I looked around for a while, and then I walked up to the desk.

"You got any books about building ramps?" I asked.

The woman, glasses slipping down her nose, looked over the desk at me. "A ramp?"

I nodded.

Her head, covered with tight brown curls, moved a bit, an uncertain tilt like she thought I'd said something unworthy of a library. She didn't say another word, took a few moments to finish whatever it was she was doing, and then she led me over to a bookshelf across the room, pulled out several books, flipped through a couple, replaced them.

"Let's see," she said, pushing her glasses up on her nose, nodding as if she'd just struck pay dirt. "Levers, pulleys, springs, screws, wheels and axles, inclined planes, and wedges. This ought to do it." She shut the book and said, "You might try *Popular Mechanics*. It's a magazine, so you can't check it out, but you could make Xerox copies if you found something."

I wasn't sure I had time so I told her this would do for now. We returned to the desk, I checked out the book, and she handed it over. "You be sure and wear a helmet, now, okay?" Her smile was more stern than friendly.

That afternoon when Buddy came home he was full of more stories. He said that Evel Knievel was setting up some reserved rooms at the Blue Lakes Inn for when he was in town, that he'd be popping in now and then to get things set up, check out the developments at the site. He wasn't always publicizing when he was here, but Buddy and the others working for Evel would know.

"It's all hush, hush," he told us. "Drinking a bit over there at the Holiday Inn across the street when he's in town." He laughed. "Boy, the women. Don't know where these women are coming from, maybe California, with movie star looks, all gorgeous, hanging around the Holiday Inn when Evel's in town. Blondes, girls with—" He paused, glanced over at Grandma, who just shook her head.

"We got plenty of pretty girls here," Grandma Grace said, "without having to import them, Buddy."

He laughed.

Sunday morning, we went to Mass, then Buddy asked Grandma Grace if he could borrow the car and take me over to the pool for a swim. He didn't have to report until late that evening.

"He's been invited to go with the Edsen kids tomorrow," Grandma told him.

"What? A kid can't go swimming two days in a row? It's summer, Mom."

"Okay, okay," she said with a wave of her hand. "Might give me a chance to get something done without you two boys underfoot."

I ran back to my room to get my swimming trunks, and we took off.

I didn't even know where the pool was, but Mrs. Edsen said we could ride our bikes so I figured it wasn't that far. After we'd gone a ways, I saw the big line of familiar poplar trees, and I knew we were headed out of town.

"Where are we going?" I asked Buddy.

He grinned and said, "Need to drop by work first."

Well, I had no idea what that meant. *Work?* But then, I remembered that Grandma Grace said when Evel wasn't in town, Buddy was guarding the site. We were going to the site! In the newspaper that morning, it said that Evel had been in town, and I asked Buddy and he said it was true, but he'd been in for the day, then out. He'd come in mostly to ease the town's jitters, talk to the newspaper people, just a visit between his ongoing events and his big promotional tour, calling a press conference to let the town folks know that he would handle things, take care of all their concerns.

When we crossed over the Perrine Bridge, which spanned the canyon alongside another bridge under construction to replace the old one that Buddy said had been there since 1927, I knew I'd been mistaken because we were headed to the north side of the canyon and the jump site was on the south. We turned right off the highway onto a dirt road, then another, then over sagebrush and rocks, Buddy throwing me one of his playful grins now and then. A large bird flew overhead, casting a shadow, and I guessed it was a hawk, or eagle. Or maybe some kind of flesh-eating bird, a carnivore like a vulture, scouting out the flat dusty earth below looking for something to eat. Dirt flew up, coating the sides of the car, and I wondered if Buddy didn't realize Grandma Grace might find it a tad bit suspicious coming back from the pool in a filthy car. I understood, though Buddy hadn't told me, that we weren't going to tell Grandma Grace about this little side trip on our way to the pool.

Finally we stopped. Buddy motioned me to hop out.

"Watch out for rattlesnakes," he cautioned me.

"Really?" I asked, thinking maybe he was kidding.

"Just listen," Buddy told me, "and you'll hear if one is about to strike. You'll definitely know when those rattles get going. Keep an eye and ear open. Okay?"

"Yep, okay." It was darn hot out there, the midday Idaho sun beating down on the desert. I wished I'd put on my swimming trunks before we left, but we were in a hurry to get going and I didn't want to give Grandma Grace time to think about it and change her mind, so I was wearing my long pants. My good pants, the ones I'd worn to church. I stepped carefully, cautiously through the sagebrush, a strong, unmistakable Idaho scent blowing in the breeze, and I was watching so close, keeping my eyes and ears tight to the ground, that it came as a surprise when we approached the canyon.

Buddy pointed directly across the wide gap, but he hardly had to. There it stood, looking as big as an Egyptian pyramid even from the distance.

"The ramp," I said.

"A bit of a dirt pile right now, but the engineers are working on getting the launch ramp just right. It's all about the angles. Have to have a perfect angle on that launch to make it across. Skycycle 2 is still in California, more engineers working on it."

"Skycycle?" I asked. "It's not really a motorcycle, is it?"

"Not really," he said. "It's more like a rocket, with steam engine propulsion. But it's going to be risky. From what I'm hearing, Evel won't have much control. He'll just be sitting. No steering device."

"So, it just shoots over the canyon with him inside?"

"Pretty much."

"Skycycle 2?"

"They launched one, a test, last November. They've been working on this for a while. Started out with a different design engineer. Don't think he and Evel got along. He brought in this Bob Truax. Evel says he's worked with the U. S. space program. The guy knows what he's doing."

Sounded like they were building a rocket for sure, I thought, not a motorcycle.

I took a cautious step and gazed down at the steep drop, over dark, sharp columns of rock, looking like nature's own temple, then down toward the bottom where broken lava rocks lay piled in heaps. The Snake River, hundreds of feet below, wound through the canyon with graceful twists and turns looking like a slimy green snake slithering down in that gorge. Lava rocks, some jagged and spiky, others all worn down like teeth in an ancient monster's mouth that had already eaten a man or two alive made me wonder if it'd leave him all bloody and mangled, bones crushed, if he crashed and didn't make it over. If he landed in the river I figured he was a dead man, too.

"The property on this side is owned by the government," Buddy said, looking down, then glancing behind us. "Evel is attempting to get rights for the landing. No problem on the launch site since it's privately owned and he's paid a tidy sum for the use."

"Do you think he can? Get the rights from the government?" I remembered that Ricky said he couldn't jump the Grand Canyon because the government wouldn't let him.

"Don't know," Buddy said after a few thoughtful moments. "I imagine the man will do it with or without."

I didn't know if Buddy meant he'd try jumping even if he didn't get the rights, or if he thought he'd actually make it across the canyon.

Buddy walked a little closer, looked down. I stood behind

him, not wanting to go any farther.

"Do they call it the Snake," I asked, "because it's all windy like a snake, or because of all the rattlesnakes around here?" I glanced behind us, then down at my feet, feeling doubly threatened now that we'd reached our destination of the canyon's edge, which was one heck of a long, steep, rocky drop.

"From what I understand," Buddy said, "it has something to do with a hand sign,"—he made an S-shape with his fingers—"that the Shoshone Indians used in describing the river to the early explorers. The sign represented the swimming salmon that inhabited the river back then, but the white men thought they were calling it the snake, and that's how it got its name."

"Shoshone Indians? Like Shoshone Falls down there?" My eyes scanned the bottom of the canyon, then along the south side, but I couldn't make out the falls because of the way the walls of the canyon twisted and turned off to the east.

Buddy pointed. "Better to view it from the other side, or better yet go right down into the canyon."

"Mom took me," I said, "down to see the Shoshone Falls." Buddy was staring down, his eyes fixed, then darting as if searching for something lost. For a very brief moment I thought he might fly right off the edge. He was quiet for a long, long moment.

"You miss her?" he asked, finally looking at me.

I just nodded and took a step back.

"Things she's got to do, Pick." He stepped back too. "She'll be back for you." He ruffled my hair, which was already being whipped up by the wind, noticeably stronger as we'd approached the canyon's rim.

We walked back to the car. As we drove out to the highway, Buddy said, "You know how long I've lived here?"

I shrugged.

"All my life, twenty-one years. Well, some time up at U of I, but this has always been home. And you know, in all that time, I've never once seen a rattler on the north side at that particular point." He laughed. "But that doesn't mean they're not there."

After driving over more sage and sand and dust, bumps and holes, and rocky unpaved roads as well as past lazy-eyed cattle, grazing on tufts of what looked like inedible thistle, we arrived at an area that actually had some small twisted trees, a bit of green, a patch of water here and there.

"Don't do much but graze on this side," Buddy explained. "The soil's too shallow for farming." He pointed back to where we'd been, across the canyon, then into the middle distance. "Potato farms out there. Of course, you've heard about our famous potatoes."

"Yep," I said as we approached the gate to the site. With little more than a Buddy grin, the guard, a fellow in jeans, dirty T-shirt and dusty white cowboy hat with a wad of chew in his cheek, waved us through. We parked and again Buddy motioned me out. He knew all the other guards and we got to get up real close to the launch ramp, which was just one big old wedge of dry desert dirt with a metal launch pad that sat at an angle that looked like it could shoot a rocket straight to heaven.

"How's he going to get up there?" I asked.

"With a great deal of show," Buddy said. "I'll guarantee you that. Evel doesn't do anything without putting on a show." Grandma had used the same word. A *show*. I wondered if Buddy could get me in without a ticket. I knew the tickets were going for twenty-five dollars and there was no way I'd have that kind of money. I knew Grandma Grace wouldn't pay.

We walked around the site a bit, Buddy pointing out Shoshone Falls, which was easier to see from this side. Even from this distance it was impressive, and I thought I could hear the muffled thunder as it cascaded over the giant basalt rocks.

Buddy stopped and talked to some of the other guards.

"Day off, Buddy?" one of them asked.

"Coming in later. Just showing my nephew—this is Pick," he introduced me. "He's visiting from out of town."

"Well, hope you'll be around for the jump," another guard, a fellow in dusty blue jeans and a straw farmer's hat with a feather in the brim, said.

I didn't say anything but I nodded as if to say yes, then glanced again at Buddy who didn't say a word either.

We hopped back into Grandma's now-filthy car and headed back over the bumpy path onto the main road into town.

"You know, Pick, if you'd chosen it yourself," Buddy said, "a summer to be here in Twin, you couldn't have found a better one. The summer of '74 is about as exciting a time as any ten-year-old kid could ask for." He looked over at me, pushed his thick, black, windblown hair back off his forehead and grinned, and I knew he was right.

When we got back into town, we drove the car through a car wash, dried it, even vacuumed and cleaned off the inside too with a cloth Grandma Grace kept in the jockey box. The desert dust had managed to seep through, leaving a layer on the dash and door handles and car mats. Then we went over to Harmon Park. It was a big pool, painted blue on the bottom so the water looked like a clear, refreshing, untouched mountain lake, other than the fact it was jam-packed full of kids. Buddy gave me a dollar, said it would be enough for getting in and buying a candy bar and pop, then told me he'd be back to pick me up in an hour.

"You're not going?" I asked, disappointed and a little scared.

"Bunch of kids," he said. The pool was surrounded by a chain link fence that you could see right through, so I knew what Buddy said was true. Mostly kids, a few parents since it was Sunday, but nobody cool like Buddy. There was a covered area on one side of the pool for people to sit and watch, and I could see that was mostly grownups, moms and dads. I wished Buddy would stay and watch. I didn't want to be there all alone.

I went inside, paid, and the girl taking the money handed me a bag on a hanger where she said I could put my clothes. "Pin this to your suit," she explained, fingering a metal tag on a safety pin attached to the bag.

In the men's locker room, I put on my swimming trunks,

36

pinned the tag on my suit, returned the bag with my clothes, undershorts tucked in the pocket of what I now realized were fairly dirty church pants, having walked through the north side desert as well as the site in them, and then I went out to the pool. I looked around hoping to see someone I knew, knowing there were only a few people in this whole town I even knew, then eased myself into the shallow end.

The water was freezing, but after a while I decided if I dunked my whole body in I'd get used to it, so I did. I walked out a little toward the deep end until I could barely touch, then attempted to swim across. It was a huge pool, pretty far from one side to the other, and I had to stop once before I made it all the way. The deep end was roped off and there were two diving boards, a short one, and one that must have been at least ten or twelve feet high. Some teenagers were diving from the high board. A guy about fourteen did a flip like he was competing for a spot on the Olympic team. Lifeguards sat up on high chairs with umbrellas. It looked like the biggest part of their job was yelling at kids, and testing others to see if they were okay to swim in the deep end. You had to be able to swim the entire width to be allowed in the deep end. I resigned myself to being stuck here with the kiddies, not that I really wanted to go out into the deep end anyway. I wondered if Ricky was a good swimmer, if he'd be out in the deep end, if he'd laugh at me because I couldn't swim across without stopping.

I tried again, making it three-quarters over. So I kept practicing, trying to find a clear path from one side to the other, bumping into a kid now and then, since the pool was filling up with more and more kids. Several times I stopped to rest, hanging near the roped-off deep end, watching the divers. Finally, about half an hour into the hour, I made it across the pool. I thought about asking the lifeguard for a test, so I could go over to the deep end with Ricky tomorrow. I wondered if you had to take the test every time you came, or if the lifeguards would know. It wasn't like they were passing out certificates or anything.

I swam back over to the rope, looked up at the nearest lifeguard, a guy with big muscles and a deep tan, perched on his stand a bit over from the rope, but I couldn't work up the nerve to ask for a test. It appeared you actually had to take the test in the deep end, which made me wonder—what if you failed the test? What if you only made it half way? Would the lifeguard come in after you? So far, I hadn't seen anyone fail the test.

I stood near the rope and looked up toward the high diving board. A blond girl in a red bathing suit was climbing up. She walked gracefully to the end of the board. Something about her seemed familiar and I realized that she was the babysitter from City Park, the girl on the picnic bench reading the book. In a bathing suit she looked even more beautiful. She raised her hands above her head in perfect formation, and then launched into the pool. I don't know that I've ever seen anything quite so beautiful as that girl in the red bathing suit, diving into the pool. When she surfaced again she was smiling. I remembered what Grandma Grace had told Buddy. *We've got plenty of pretty girls around here.* At least one perfect girl, I thought, just as I heard Uncle Buddy calling my name from the observation area.

I glanced up at the clock hanging on the building where the lockers were located, and I couldn't believe an hour had passed. I hadn't even stopped to get a candy bar.

On the way home, munching the Three Musketeers I'd picked up on the way out, I told Buddy thank you.

"Happy to do it," he said. "Probably be more fun tomorrow with Ricky. Always more fun with a friend."

"Yep," I said, wondering if it was really true—not about the more fun, but about the friend.

My mom called that night. She said she was settled in an apartment, that she was excited about starting work on Monday. When she asked what I'd been doing I said I'd gone to lunch with Grandma Grace at Crowley's and had a chocolate milkshake and one of those giant cheeseburgers, made some new friends, gone to the library, helped with curtains for the bedroom, gone swimming at Harmon Park. I didn't tell her that Buddy had taken me out to the launch site as well as the landing site for Evel Knievel's jump across the Snake River Canyon. Somehow I understood that was between me and Buddy.

She said, "Wow, sounds like you've been keeping pretty busy and having lots of fun."

And I said, "Yeah."

Ricky and Danny had swimming lessons again Monday morning, but after lunch, Ricky and I rode our bikes to Harmon Park. His friend Jeff, a tall lanky kid with a goofy smile, half teeth, half gums, came along too. Grandma Grace had decided I could have a dollar a week for allowance, so I'd have enough for some snacks too. The chore list she'd left for me that morning included taking my church pants out in the back yard and shaking them out real good to get the dust off before I put them in the hamper. I'd slept late so hadn't seen her that morning. I wondered if she was going to be upset, or ask where the heck I'd been to get them so dirty. She'd seemed real pleased when Buddy and I got back from the pool and Buddy told her we'd run the car through the car wash. Grandma Grace said she'd got a lot done without us hanging around bothering her. When I went into my bedroom, I saw new pillows on the beds. She'd dyed the bedspreads brown. They looked pretty good.

We took a different way to the park than Buddy and I had when we came from the canyon. I told Ricky and Jeff about Buddy being Evel Knievel's bodyguard, about him taking me to the site. Ricky commented again that Buddy was cool, and Jeff asked if I'd met Evel Knievel, and I told them how he was going on a promotional tour, going all over the country, but he'd made a quick stop here a couple of days ago. Jeff, said, yeah, he knew, his dad had read it in the newspaper. Neither of them asked how Buddy could be his bodyguard if he wasn't even here.

I told them Buddy was going to take me to the jump, though he hadn't told me that at all. They both said I was really lucky, that they wished they could go, too.

I told them it cost twenty-five dollars, and Jeff let out a whistle like there was no way either of them could come up with that kind of money.

We zipped down streets, not even stopping when we came to the busy intersections with stop signs, just darting around cars, through a narrow little street that looked more like an alley, past baseball diamonds at the park. We stopped once inside the park, before we got to the pool. A wide ditch with fast-flowing water wound right through the park. A bunch of tough-looking kids, older than us, probably twelve, stood around the "coulee," as Jeff called it, with their bikes. They'd set up a ramp, that looked a lot better than ours, and I could see one of the biggest boys was going to jump. He did a couple circles around on the grass, then turned, pedaled faster and faster as he approached the ramp, flying in the air once he launched. I could see right away he wasn't going to make it. Plop, with a loud splash, he was in the coulee, trying desperately to hang onto his bike. The water's current was powerful, and I felt a rush of heat, then a cold trickle like melting ice run down my back as the kid's head bobbed up and down even as he attempted to get a grip on his bike. His friends rushed to the rescue, grabbing his arm, yanking him out. He coughed and spit, doubled over, but didn't seem to be hurt. The bike floated down a bit, then lodged on the bank of the coulee and a couple other boys yanked it up by the slippery handlebars and pulled it out.

A good-sized crowd had gathered now and someone yelled, "Who do you think you are? Evel Knievel?"

"You think that's the Snake River Canyon?" someone else shouted.

Everybody laughed, including Ricky, Jeff, and me, feeling safe to do that now that the boy and bike had been retrieved.

One of the boy's friends glared over at us—me, Ricky, and Jeff, standing, straddling our bikes. Jeff was still grinning, but both Ricky and I had wiped any trace of making or having fun off our faces. Jeff, I could see, was one of those kids who smiled when he was nervous, and it was like that grin had frozen there from fear. His hands were doing an anxious little dance along his handlebars. The bigger boy's dark eyes did a quiet sweep over the three of us as he swaggered toward us, nostrils flaring. He stopped and his eyes locked with mine, then slid along my bike. "That your grandpa's bike?" he snarled.

I knew my bike wasn't cool like most of the other boys, but neither Ricky nor Jeff had said anything, as if some of Uncle Buddy's cool had rubbed off on me. Obviously this guy didn't know Uncle Buddy. Quickly, the three of us hopped on our bikes and sped off toward the pool, not even riding on the path, but bumping along the grass, glancing back to see if anyone was after us. The boy who'd fallen in was wringing out his shirt. The boy who'd yelled at me was kicking the ramp to adjust its position to take another shot at the coulee. They'd lost interest in us, the uninvited, and probably not-very-intimidating, novice hecklers.

At the pool, Jeff and Ricky headed right to the deep end, and didn't even consider that maybe I shouldn't go with them. So I just followed along, jumped right in. I felt my body go deeper and deeper, a bit of panic running again along my spine like it had when the boy and his bike hit the coulee, but I was pretty sure I'd come back up, and I did. We spent the afternoon in the deep end, jumping off the low board that wasn't even that scary after the first few times. Swimming from the place you landed off the board back to the edge to get out and do it again wasn't hard at all. The lifeguard didn't ask me to take the test. I think the thing I learned that afternoon—if you act like you know what you're doing, everybody thinks you do.

Ricky's mom never did show up with Danny, so about four o'clock, when Jeff said he had to go home, we hopped on our bikes.

At dinner that evening, Buddy had more stories. He said the jump was going to be shown on closed-circuit TV, that it

41

wouldn't be on real TV, that people could pay all over the country to go to a movie theater to watch. Evel had hired this big promotion company.

"Top Rank out of New York," he explained. "Same company that does all the big fights, like the Mohammad Ali-Frazier bout at Madison Square Garden." He glanced over at Grandma Grace, like she knew all about Top Rank and boxing. "At ten dollars a shot for that closed-circuit TV playing in theaters all over the world, they'll be hauling in truckloads of money."

"Ten dollars?" Grandma Grace asked as if she couldn't believe anyone would pay such a price. "A fool and his money are soon parted. A lot of money to pay for a show that will last about two minutes at the most."

Buddy told us that's why they were lining up all kinds of performances for the canyon's edge the day of the jump that would be shown on the closed-circuit TV in the theaters to make a big and lengthy movie-house-worthy production out of it, though he figured people would pay big bucks just to see the jump.

"The famous Karl Wallenda will do a tightrope walking trick," he said, "a blindfolded motorcycle stuntman is going to ride along the canyon's edge. There'll be some motocross races, too, with big money prizes."

"Let's hope this doesn't turn into the Idaho version of Woodstock," Grandma Grace said, shaking her head. "Naked hippies dancing all over the place."

I didn't say a word, didn't move, but I felt my face muscles twitching and working toward a grin. I'd early discovered if I was quiet and still the adults would forget I was there and just keep on talking and telling.

"Tim Qualls says he's no Max Yasgur," Buddy said. "This isn't going to be a rock fest." He laughed. "Earlier they brought some rock show promoter in from California to see if something like that might work. You know what he said?"

"I can only imagine," Grandma Grace replied as she got up

to start clearing the dinner dishes off the table, as if she'd had enough Evel Knievel talk for the day.

"He said this was no place for a rock show. Town of 16,000 at the most."

"Did this big rock music promoter come in and count them?" Grandma Grace asked. "I think we've got a few more than that." She sounded almost defensive.

"And he said we had no roads. No hotels. No place to eat."

No place to poop, either, I thought, bringing my hand to my mouth to catch the laugh I felt coming.

"But there's going to be concessions," Buddy went on, "souvenirs, hot dogs, hamburgers, sodas and beer. Opportunities for people in the community to make some money. Evel will take his cut, being the businessman he is."

"Well, that's a good combination," Grandma Grace snorted, "a bunch of crazies, hanging on the canyon's edge, drinking beer. How many tickets they selling? I heard numbers like half a million, then two hundred thousand. Can you imagine? People'll be falling into the canyon, killing themselves. Is that really what Twin Falls wants to be known for?"

"Out of consideration for the town," Buddy said, more like he was explaining facts, rather than defending, "he's agreed to limit ticket sales to 50,000."

"Oh, good," Grandma Grace said. "That'll only double and a half the population." She popped a Tupperware lid on the bowl she'd just scraped some leftovers into and slid it into the fridge. "You know, Buddy, the President of the United States of America has been accused of lying and cheating, with that Watergate problem, probably be impeached, thrown out of office, and here we are, spending our dinner table time, talking about Evel Knievel."

Buddy didn't say more, just looked down at the ice cream he'd scooped into his dessert bowl, shook his head, attempting to stifle his grin. And so did I.

The following morning, Grandma Grace came in and woke me up and told me she had another job for me, something that could keep me busy in the mornings, but she had to explain, not just put it into a note. She took me into her room and showed me a stack of fabric, some of the prints we'd picked out together for the quilts, some she already had—one of them being the fabric with the colorful sports balls, the one I'd cut a jagged hole right into the middle.

"It's easy," she said, showing me a pattern, which was nothing more than a paper square. "Cut the fabric into squares. Then I'll sew them together for the quilts. Don't waste any. Don't go leaving big gaps between the squares. Cut real straight." She demonstrated how to line the square pattern up against the smoothest, straightest edge, pin it to the fabric, then cut. If I cut very straight, the side on the first square would be the side for the next square. "If you get to the end of the material and you can't fit in another square, that's fine. We'll save the smaller pieces for something else." I'd already figured out that Grandma Grace wasn't wasteful. You didn't throw away stuff that could be used, or in the case of food, eaten later.

Well, I wasn't too happy about this whole project, though it seemed rather simple. I wondered what Ricky and Jeff would think if they knew I was helping my grandmother make quilts. Though she didn't ask me to do any sewing, at least at that point, I didn't think making quilts was a thing a man, or even a boy, should do. But, at the same time, I realized if I cut that sports-ball fabric up into squares, she'd never know I'd snipped that piece out of the center when I thought she was going to make me another pair of pajamas.

Before she took off for work, Grandma Grace looked me over real good, touched my cheek, twisted my head, then lifted my chin and said, "You been putting on that ChapStick? Your lips, your skin look much better."

I gave her a vague nod, more of a chin to shoulder, not really a yes, because I didn't want to lie and I was just agreeing that they were doing better. I hadn't been using the ChapStick or lotion at all since my mom left, but Grandma Grace's asking made me realize that my mouth and dry cheeks and chin were doing better. And it dawned on me that my body, if not my mind, was actually getting used to this place where humidity was close to zero, making some kind of adjustment all on its own.

After I finished my regular chores, I started in on the fabric. I turned on the TV and sat clipping away with my scissors, watching some quiz shows, stacking the fabric in neat little square piles, even matching them up in colors that seemed to go together, the way I'd seen Grandma Grace do. I finished the sports-ball fabric and stuffed the uneven leftovers in the bottom of the kitchen garbage can, then decided I'd take it out to the alley and dump it. I was the only one taking out garbage now, so I felt confident that Grandma Grace would never know.

That afternoon I went over to Ricky's, knocked on the back door and asked his mom, who answered, if he could play. She went to get him and within seconds he bounded out, and we rushed to the garage to work on the ramp. I'd looked at the book the lady at the library had found for me, but it didn't seem to be much help. The ramp, according to the book, was an inclined plane, but it said nothing about riding bikes or motorcycles, or jumping garbage cans or trucks or cars or coulees or canyons. It didn't help at all with how to put a ramp together, to know the right angle, the measurements or proportions of the pieces to support the ramp, or secure it.

I told Ricky, who seemed to think we should continue with our original plan, that it looked like the boys at Harmon Park had cut the pieces for the sides out of plywood too, that the ramp wasn't as wide and bulky as ours which made it much easier to transport, otherwise how could they have hauled it over to the park? I didn't want to say it was a better ramp than ours, but I think Ricky could see that.

"But it didn't work," he said. "Dumped that kid right in the coulee." We both laughed.

"Maybe that had something do with his riding skills," I added, "or his not having any."

"That's for sure," Ricky said. He paused for a moment as if considering. "You can borrow my bike when we get ready to jump."

Neither he nor Jeff had said anything about my second-hand bike, Buddy's leftover, fixed-up bike, not even after the kid at the park had made fun of me. But it was pretty obvious that it wasn't a jumping bike. I felt embarrassed, but knew Ricky was just being nice, so I said thank you.

"We're leaving tomorrow for the Fourth of July," Ricky told me. "Going to my grandma and grandpa's cabin in the mountains. Garbageman won't even come this week because of the holiday. Won't be here 'til next week."

I still didn't quite understand why we could only attempt the jump after the garbage man came. So what if the garbage cans had garbage in them—they all had lids.

Buddy wasn't on a regular schedule now—he was at Evel's beck-and-call as Grandma described it—so sometimes he didn't make it home for dinner, but when he did, he always had something to share. I felt like I had a front-row seat for everything that was leading up to the big event.

"Evel's invited Elvis to come to the jump, invited Mrs. Kennedy and Aristotle Onassis, and Liz Taylor, and even Steve McQueen." I knew Steve McQueen was a TV and movie star who was also known for his motorcycle riding skills.

"He even invited the Pope," Buddy said glancing at Grandma to catch her reaction.

Grandma's laugh came out more through her nose than her mouth. "Well, that might be worth getting a ticket for," she replied, real serious like, though I could tell she was making fun. She always listened, though, to what Buddy said. Grandma Grace pooh-poohed just about everything he told us, but she was listening. Like me, she was taking in every little detail.

46

Buddy told us Evel Knievel was going home to Butte for the Fourth of July holiday before the big kickoff of his thirty-nine-city promotional tour. He was going to be the Grand Marshall of the Independence Day holiday parade. Buddy said he was also still doing some special jumps around the country prior to his canyon jump.

"What if he gets hurt?" I asked. "What if he is hurt too bad to do the canyon jump?"

"Ah," Buddy answered, "they'll stick in some metal pieces, put him back together. Half his body's metal now anyway. He won't let us down. Evel's a man of his word. Keeps his promises."

Grandma just rolled her eyes.

There wasn't much going on in Twin Falls for the Fourth of July, not a parade, not even official city fireworks, though Grandma Grace said they used to do that over at the ballpark when the town had a real baseball team. Buddy said there would be plenty of fireworks, and Grandma Grace shook her head and said, "Of the illegal type."

Buddy worked late on the Fourth, so I went with Grandma Grace for a drive and picnic to the Thousand Springs with a couple of her widow friends from church. Pretty boring except for the food—fried chicken, potato salad, Jell-O salad with fruit cocktail and whipped cream, chocolate cake, and pop and lemonade. That evening we went to a band concert in City Park where they played all kinds of patriotic songs, like Yankee Doodle Dandy. Later, after Grandma and I went to bed, Buddy came in, woke me up, and took me outside and we shot off some fireworks and lit some sparklers. I could tell he'd been drinking because he smelled of beer. We could hear fireworks going off all over town. After a while, Grandma Grace came out, tying the belt of her robe, hair up in curlers, and told us we better not burn down the neighborhood. By then we were about done with the bag of celebrating Buddy had brought home anyway.

The day after the Fourth, Grandma Grace asked me if I

wanted to go to the hospital to visit the pediatric ward. She'd finished sewing the quilts made out of the squares I'd cut. She said I'd done a fine job and liked the way I'd matched up the colors. She said I had a real eye.

When we got there, we nearly ran into a kid zooming down the hall on a tricycle. He looked pretty healthy, except for the fact that he didn't have any hair. Another kid sat with his mom in what looked like a playroom, trying to put together a puzzle with just one arm. Well, he had two, but one was in a cast.

We checked in at the nurses' station, and the nurse, a pretty lady with reddish hair, smiled and smiled and carried on about how much all the children, as well as the parents and hospital staff, appreciated Grandma Grace. When Grandma introduced me, the nurse's grin grew even wider, though I didn't think that was possible. It really did seem to stretch from ear to ear and she had very large teeth and very red lipstick that framed her friendly grin. She helped us carry a stack of quilts around to the various rooms, where anxious parents sat beside sick children—the ones in the beds, not the ones terrorizing the place and screaming down the halls. Some of them looked pretty sick. The place smelled all mediciney, and I just wanted to leave, but I kept going, wondering if I should really be getting all this credit for being such a good kid when I really, really didn't want to be there. As we distributed the quilts, letting the kids pick their favorites, the smiley, red-headed nurse kept telling me how special this was for me to come with my grandma, who told the lady proudly that I'd also helped make the quilts.

When we got home I went out to the patio and sat, staring out at the alley, wishing that Ricky would be home soon.

The next week when Ricky returned, Jeff and another friend named Greg, with more freckles than me and sandy-colored hair, came over and we worked on the ramp.

Greg, the newcomer, seemed eager to get things finished, but Ricky kept telling him, glancing over at me, that we had to get it right or someone might get hurt. We'd decided we did need two ramps, one for launch, one for landing, so it had turned into quite a project. Ricky had asked his dad for more boards, because we'd decided we needed to cut the sides out of plywood rather than just slap some two by fours together with nails. I wondered if his dad knew what we were doing with them. It seemed most of the parents, and in my case grandparent and uncle, were either working or busy doing something else. Whenever we went inside Ricky's house for a drink of water, or to use the bathroom, his mom was talking on the phone or watching soap operas on TV.

Garages and a few carports backed up to the alley, but as far as I could see they were used mostly for storing bikes, garden tools, and lawn mowers and other junk. Most of the neighbors parked in front of the houses on the street. Grandma Grace and Mrs. Fontinelli, a retired school teacher with hair as white and fluffy as cotton and what looked like a single bosom that stretched across the upper portion of her very stout body, were the only ones who appeared to use their garages for cars. The Allingtons at the end of the block parked their big fancy Cadillac in the garage, but had access from the street that ran perpendicular to ours, so they never drove into the alley.

I knew Grandma Grace's schedule, and she always arrived home at precisely 5:15, unless she stopped by the store or bank, which would give us extra time. Mrs. Fontinelli owned a car that looked older than cars themselves, and if she ever decided to sell it there would be no false advertising involved in claiming it was owned by a little old lady who only drove it once a week to church on Sunday.

This alley was the kingdom of kids, a place adults seldom entered, other than the garbageman who rattled down the alley once a week, lifted and dumped cans, but seemed unconcerned about any possible kids' activity or any messing around with his garbage cans. I understood it was unlikely that anyone would be coming out into the alley to dump trash in the outside metal cans right after it had been picked up.

On our next safe day, the day after the garbage pickup that week, we carried the two ramps, which we'd decided didn't have to be so wide, along with the supports, out to the alley and assembled them.

"Who's going first?" Greg asked.

"Since we built the ramp with your boards," Jeff said, "you go first." He stared directly at Ricky.

I could see Ricky didn't really want to go first, but after a moment, he hopped on his bike, circled a couple of times around the ramp and four garbage cans, then pedaled slowly down to the end of the alley as if he was going to try it. But instead he rode back up next to the ramp. "Let's try three at first," he suggested. He hopped off his bike, and we pulled one of the garbage cans to the side.

He rode his bike down the alley again, turned around, lined it up in a straight line with the ramp, and then, head down, started forward as fast as he could. He hit the ramp solidly and it didn't give or buckle, just as we'd hoped. He launched into the air smooth as can be, flew over the three garbage cans, made a perfect landing on the second ramp, wobbled a little, but held tight as he continued down the alley. I'd never expected that from a pudgy kid I'd called a pig before we got to be friends, and I thought how people often aren't what you think they are. Several yards from the landing ramp, he let out a triumphant holler, and then turned, sliding along, spraying up a cloud of dust and alley rocks.

"Good jump," Jeff yelled. "My turn."

As if we'd established a hierarchy, based on the order in which we had come to the project, Jeff prepared, without further discussion, lining up at the far end of the alley, and then taking off. Not as perfect as Ricky's run—his foot slid off the pedal—but he made an adjustment just in time and didn't crash.

"You're up, Pick," Ricky said, tapping his handlebar, offering his bike to me. I was shaking a bit, scared I wouldn't make it, that I'd crash, end up all cut and bruised, wreck my friend's bike. For a second I thought about telling Greg to go next, but in a sense I knew it was my turn, that I'd become part of this foursome, not even relegated to last.

"I'll use my bike," I said with a laugh. "If I crash, I'll borrow yours." Nobody else laughed. I think they all thought maybe on the big old heavy bike of Buddy's, with those humongous tires, I was sure to crash.

I started down to the end of the alley, turned slowly. Stopped and straddled my bike for a moment of reflection, then hopped back on and pedaled as fast as I could. I hit the ramp much harder than I'd hoped, felt a bump, a nervous lump of something inside me ready to jump right out of my gut into my throat as I launched into the air. For one beautiful moment, I was flying. I was in the air, one with my bike, flying. I cleared the garbage cans by a good foot, landing on the far edge of the landing ramp, not smooth by any means, but I didn't fly off the bike as I continued down the alley. When finally I slowed, feeling very much in control, I glanced back and thought, *I can do four.* Yes, I can easily clear four garbage cans.

I wondered if my size, my lack of weight, worked sort of like a jockey on a horse. I was so much smaller than the other boys, my bike so much larger, yet I'd done just fine.

Greg's attempt was not as graceful as Ricky's, or even as controlled as Jeff's, or as far as mine. His back tire hit the third garbage can, having launched off the ramp too soon. His bike slid on its side, causing Greg to skid along the alley, even as he held tight. He was wearing long jeans, so there was no real damage, but he was pretty shook up.

As we gathered for a conference of sorts, all of us ready to add one more garbage can, Jeff's mom hollered down the alley from his back yard.

"Don't do it without me," he implored.

"We won't," Ricky said, eyes darting around the circle. So we carried the pieces back to the garage. We all knew we were ready to try four.

I dreamed about it that night. It felt good, that feel of flying. That feel of having no control whatsoever, but at the same time feeling you controlled the world, that one false move, one turn of the handle, one false landing, you'd be skidding along the alley, crashing your head against one of the backyard fences or one of the makeshift wooden stands that held the garbage cans.

On the days we didn't work on the ramp or jump, there was plenty to do. Ricky, Jeff, and I would go on long bike rides, hang around at City Park, climbing on a big pile of lava rocks, then running around on the bandshell stage, making up songs and performances as if we were in a rock band. Sometimes Greg would go, too. We'd play baseball in an empty lot, or go watch Greg, who played over at Harmon Park on an official team, though he wasn't very good and sat on the bench most of the time.

We found a pond and caught frogs, and we built a fort in Ricky's backyard and slept in it one night, telling scary stories and eating cookies that Jeff had sneaked out of his pantry. About midnight we got up, crept into the alley, then along the fences, peering into windows, though there was nothing to see since even the adults had turned out the lights and gone to bed. In the morning, the air was as cool and damp as a defrosting freezer. We went inside Ricky's house and loaded bowls with breakfast cereal and made chocolate milk, then went back to our fort and huddled in our blankets, making plans for the day.

We swam at Harmon Park. There was plenty to do besides jumping garbage cans. And Grandma Grace kept me busy in the mornings with her list of chores. I was now doing some of the things that Buddy had done before he got a job, like mowing the lawn. Grandma said she'd give me an extra dollar for that, and also suggested I go over and see if I could help Mrs. Fontinelli who spent a lot of time in her yard with her gardens. Mrs. Fontinelli said she'd pay me to do some weeding, and asked me what grade I was in, what was my favorite subject—I told her math—sounding very much like the retired school teacher she was. She paid me a penny per weed.

"Math?" she asked.

"Yep."

"You can always use math. What would you like to pursue when you're out of school?"

"Guess I haven't thought that far ahead."

"I taught English."

I wasn't sure what I was supposed to say about that, so I didn't say a thing. English had never been my favorite.

Mrs. Fontinelli sat in a metal lawn chair, supervising my weed pulling, but I got the idea she just wanted to talk, that maybe she was lonely.

"Your mom was always a good student."

I knew my mom was smart, but she never went to college.

"Buddy, too," she said thoughtfully. "I hope he can go back to college. He's a smart boy. He used to come in after class sometimes. I think he was embarrassed to ask questions in class, a little shy, but a very inquisitive, smart boy. Your Grandma says he's having a rough time now. Girl problems." She paused as if I could fill her in on Buddy's problems, but I didn't know a thing, other than what I'd accidentally heard my mom and Grandma talking about.

"He's working for Evel Knievel," I told her, "making money so he can go back to school."

"Evel Knievel?" she asked. "Well, isn't that something. Happy to hear Buddy will continue his education."

With the money I was making with chores and jobs, now I could go swimming at least twice a week and still get snacks every time.

Toward the end of the month, we'd perfected our ramp, our individual jumping techniques and we'd moved on to jumping four garbage cans at a time.

Late one morning, we lined up the ramp, pulled out four

garbage cans, and then one by one we all gave it a try, each of us making it with various levels of coordination and control.

Ricky said. "I think it's too easy."

"Let's do five!" Jeff exclaimed.

We lined the fifth up, adjusted the ramps.

Again, Ricky flew over, wobbling a bit against the landing ramp, but not losing control.

Jeff went next and hit his back tire on the fourth can, went flying off the side of the ramp, crashed his bike.

We all gasped.

Jeff stood, shook his head, rubbed his side. "I'm okay," he told us. He was grinning that big nervous grin of his and for a moment I thought he was going to burst out in tears. But I could see he wasn't going to let this get the best of him.

"I want a turn," a small voice cried out. We all turned to see Ricky's little brother Danny, who oddly hadn't been hanging around much, and even when he did we could usually get rid of him without much trouble. Whenever he threatened to tell his mom, Ricky would bring up something Danny had done that his mom didn't know about.

"You'll get hurt," Jeff said. "I barely made it."

"I'm telling Mom," Danny screamed.

"Okay," Ricky said, "but just one can."

Jeff, Greg and I exchanged glances. We all figured he'd crash, run in to tell his mom—if it didn't kill him—and it'd be all over for the rest of us.

Then Greg did something that saved the day. He reached into his pocket and pulled out a Tootsie Roll. Not the mini penny kind, but a full, cigar-sized Tootsie Roll, though it looked a little worn like it'd been riding around in his pocket for a while. "How about I give you this if you leave us alone?" He stooped down to Danny's face level and his voice was low, not taunting, but almost as sweet as that candy bribe he was offering.

Danny considered for a moment then reached over and took the Tootsie Roll. "Okay," he said. For some reason, I got the feeling this wasn't over yet, that we'd just begun the first stage of a bribery scheme that would continue for the rest of the summer.

After Danny left, munching on his candy, I hopped on my bike, nervous now, not so sure, thinking it would have been easier if I'd gone right after Jeff without this Danny pay-off break. But, knowing I had to do it to remain part of the gang, I lined up my bike, pedaled faster and faster down the alley. Just as my tire touched the launch ramp, I heard a familiar roar.

With his strange unscheduled schedule, you never knew when he might turn up, and though I guessed Buddy might not have a problem with what we'd been doing all summer, I hadn't told him. It was too late to stop, but the sound of Buddy's motorcycle, then seeing him stop in the alley, threw me off balance, and I knew right away I was going to crash. I didn't even make it over the fifth garbage can, my back tire hitting, throwing me like I was riding a bucking bronco, losing my grip, bike flying, me tumbling like a circus acrobat but without the necessary control. My bike crashed up against the fence to the house two down from Ricky's yard, with me skidding across the rocky alley, digging my elbow into whatever it was—something hard—underneath all those rocks. For a moment I lay there, wondering if I'd broken something, afraid to get up. When I got my bearings, stood, I could feel a sharp pain in my leg, another in my arm, nothing inside like a broken bone, but, as I glanced over my other body parts, I could see several of my fingers were cut and scraped. Blood dripped from a scrape on my elbow. I limped over to my bike and could see the tire was bent, the frame out of whack. I picked it up by the handlebars and attempted to walk it back to the ramp, but Buddy was standing in my way, looking down on me with a stern expression.

"Better put that away before your grandma sees what you boys have been doing," he said, motioning. He walked his motorcycle toward the shed and I followed, attempting to wheel my bike with its now lopsided tire as Ricky, Jeff, and Greg stood motionless in the alley, watching this parade of shame. Inside the shed Buddy instructed me to put the bike behind the wheelbarrow and some gardening supplies that I doubted anyone had used since Grandpa Jack passed away.

"What the hell have you boys been doing?" Buddy fingered his helmet, now looped on his handlebars. "Could have cracked your head wide open. Lucky it was just your bike you ruined. Goddamned stupid boys." It was strange that we'd been working on this for a good part of the summer and no one had objected, no one even seemed to be aware. And here was Buddy, the one person I thought might approve, telling me I was stupid, swearing at me even, something he didn't often do.

"How long have you been doing that?" he asked. "Looks like you put some time into building that ramp." His voice was stern, but I saw something along the line of his mouth that made me think he was about to crack a smile.

"Would have made it, if you hadn't come zooming into the alley just then. Scared me silly, threw my balance off. We're up to five garbage cans. I think I can do six," I said defiantly, not believing my nerve.

"Not with that bike," Buddy said, motioning to his old bike, which was in sorry shape.

As we walked back to the house, I glanced into the alley. My three friends were still there; they hadn't abandoned me. Ricky raised his shoulders as if to say *sorry*. We'd been caught, but at least it was Buddy, not Grandma Grace or one of the other parents. I could see they were starting to dismantle the ramp.

Inside, Buddy poured himself a glass of milk, began constructing a peanut butter sandwich, asked me if I'd had lunch. When I said no, he started making one for me too. He didn't put jelly on his peanut butter sandwiches, but he stuffed in some lettuce and I liked the taste of Buddy's peanut-butter-salad sandwiches, as he called them. Sometimes he'd fry and add some bacon, but I could see he wasn't taking time for that today.

We sat, neither of us saying anything for a while.

Finally he said, "I'll make you a deal, if you promise not to jump anymore. Your grandma and I have been talking." He paused for a long moment, took another bite of his sandwich. "You come downtown tomorrow afternoon just before Grandma Grace gets off work." He stared right at me, like he was expecting an answer to something that really wasn't a question, and he didn't say what the deal was, so I didn't know what I was agreeing to, but I nodded and said, "Okay."

The next day I had to walk downtown because I'd crashed and ruined my bike. Grandma had asked me about the Band-Aids on my fingers and I said I'd scraped them on the cupboard when I was putting away the dishes. From her raised eyebrows I could tell she didn't believe me, and I thought for a moment she might ask me how long I thought I could keep blaming that cupboard. But I didn't think Grandma Grace knew about the crash and Buddy and I had hidden the bike pretty well in the shed, which she seldom entered anyway. But I was really nervous as I walked downtown that she would ask me why I didn't ride my bike, nervous that Buddy would tell her, that she'd cut off my allowance, that I wouldn't have money to go swimming at Harmon Park anymore.

When I got there, Buddy was waiting outside. "Here's the deal, you promise not to jump and instead of that Evel Knievel stunt cycle we talked about—"

Just then, Grandma Grace walked out the front door of the J. C. Penney, pocketbook tucked under her arm.

"You ready?" She glanced from Buddy to me. She didn't mention my being bikeless. In fact, we didn't really talk, and nobody explained a thing.

We walked across the street, down the block, though I still didn't know what the deal was. We marched up to the front of the Western Auto, Buddy opened the door gallantly and the three of us walked inside. The place smelled like rubber tires, and car batteries ... and bikes! We stopped as we arrived at the floor display of shiny new bikes, all lined up, front tires set at the same angle, standing in a row like sparkling ornaments for an oversized Christmas tree. Buddy walked right over to the Western Flyer with the high handlebars like my friends, the shiny chrome, the slick new banana seat.

"Your grandma and I thought maybe this one." It was the one I would have picked myself, and I knew I must have looked as silly as that smiling nurse at the hospital. If someone had held a mirror up to my face at that moment, I would have seen my own grin stretching from ear to ear.

"You know the deal we made?" Buddy said. And I nodded in agreement.

The Western Auto man wrote up a ticket, Grandma Grace paid, pulling ones and fives and tens out of her purse, telling me that Buddy had chipped in too, and I said, "Thank you so much, Grandma Grace, thank you, Uncle Buddy."

We wheeled the bike out on the sidewalk in front of the store and Grandma Grace said, "I'll see you two boys at home."

I hopped on the bike, flying, smiling, even laughing out loud into the warm summer breeze as I sped toward home on my new Western Flyer.

After dinner that night I asked Grandma Grace if I could go show Ricky my new bike, and she said yes.

I didn't take my usual route through the alley, but went around the entire block, waving at Mrs. Fontinelli who was out working in her garden bed, and right up to the front door of Ricky's house. He answered when I rang the bell.

"You get in big trouble?" he asked with concern.

"Nope," I said. "In fact . . ." I stepped aside and held my arm out with a wide gesture like a ringmaster in a circus announcing the main event.

He glanced out to where I'd parked my new bike on the sidewalk leading up to the front porch.

"Oh, man, . . . you wreck your bike jumping and you get a brand new one?" He laughed so hard his eyes got all squinty. "How'd you do that?" They opened wide with astonishment.

"I promised Buddy I wouldn't jump anymore."

Ricky stood silently for a moment, then said, "That's okay. I think five is tops. I think we're done."

And, as easy as that, we were.

Buddy took me out to the site several times on his motorcycle—when Grandma Grace was at work, so she didn't know—insisting I wear a helmet, something he'd bought, I realized, just for me. They'd retrieved the test Skycycle that had gone into the canyon way back in November. It sat at the launch site dwarfed by that enormous ramp, appearing small and insignificant and more like a kiddy-built rocket, nothing like a motorcycle, though Evel still insisted on calling it a Skycycle. Old and rusty—maybe from being in the river for so long—it seemed more like something put together from scrap metal and old used airplane parts. I hoped the real Skycycle 2 was more impressive than this.

I was getting to know some of the other men who worked out at the site, building up fences, and a place for the press box. Evel had brought in a trailer that Buddy said he was using as a dressing room. His costumes were all part of the act. He wore white leather jumpsuits with red and blue stars and stripes to announce his patriotism and love for the U.S.A. The TV and newspaper stories called him a great American hero. He was a real-life American hero, not fake or made-up like Superman. I wondered if Evel was really going to wear one of those leather jumpsuits. It was darn hot out on that canyon rim.

One day, as we were getting back on Buddy's motorcycle, the guy who always wore the straw hat with the feather, said, "Well, I see you're still here. Guess this means you're going to stay for the big jump," and Buddy said, "Yeah, he is."

I'd told Ricky, and Jeff, and Greg I was going to the jump. Buddy had never really told me that, though the way he was always sharing details about what they were doing out at the site, the plans and development for the Skycycle, I just figured I was included. But this was the first time he actually said it. I knew

Buddy could get me into the site on September 8th to see Evel jump the Snake River Canyon, and I knew I wouldn't even need one of those twenty-five-dollar tickets.

My mom called every Sunday night. Toward the end of July she'd started talking about me coming to Seattle for school, said she was fixing a room up for me. I told her that was cool, I was excited. I asked her when school started and she said the end of August. She could drive over and get me and I could start fifth grade in Seattle. It was a nice town, everything real green, and the schools were good, she told me.

After I hung up I couldn't control the thoughts circling through my head. I missed my mom, loved my mom, and I truly wanted to be with her. But I didn't want to go to Seattle in August. I didn't want to leave Twin Falls. Not until after September 8th anyway. I'd been waiting all summer, and I didn't want to miss it. I wasn't going to miss it. But I fretted all night wondering how I could do this, how I could stay here until after Evel Knievel jumped the Snake River Canyon, without hurting my mom's feelings. And even then I knew it would involve a lie.

August was a hot month. We went swimming at least two or three times a week. We found plenty of free stuff to do, too, mostly riding bikes all over town. We could be gone all day and, as long as we were home by dinner, nobody's parents or grandparents seemed to be worried that we were getting into trouble. Buddy didn't ask me, not even once, if I'd kept my word about jumping garbage cans in the alley.

When we were at Harmon Park I always looked for the girl in the red swimming suit. I thought I might run into her again when we went over to City Park. Sometimes I thought maybe I'd made her up, or maybe if I'd see her again she wasn't really that pretty. Minds can play tricks when playing with memory, making something seem a whole lot different than it really was.

Sometimes Buddy would come home in the middle of the

morning, but I don't think he was checking up on me, because he often went to his room and took a nap, or grabbed something to eat. I guessed sometimes he'd come home at other times when I was out with my friends, because I'd see signs he'd been there—a jar of something on the counter, a few crumbs of bread, a glass or plate in the sink.

When we were both home at the same time, Grandma Grace at work, he'd tell me things about what was going on at the site or over at the Holiday Inn. I'd noticed something about Buddy as the summer progressed. After the Fourth of July, he never smelled like beer anymore when he came home. And, though Buddy's attitude was generally happy and optimistic, I could sense some worry.

"They really need more time to get the rocket ready," he told me one afternoon. "Evel was out at the site. Sat in the cockpit of the Skycycle test rocket. Pretty snug fit."

"How's he going to get out when it lands? Or if . . ."

"They're rigging up a parachute device, but he's got to get out first. I wish they had more time for development," he said with genuine concern.

"You think they'll postpone it?"

"Nope. Going off just as planned." Buddy shook his head. "Ready or not, here we come."

A couple of days later at dinner, Grandma Grace announced, "Well, I suppose you boys heard, our President resigned today. Course with all this Evel Knievel stuff going on around here, don't imagine anyone cares." She got up from the dinner table.

As she was scraping the leftovers into bowls, Buddy and I still sitting, having our dessert, a chocolate cake Grandma Grace baked the night before, she asked, "You get those papers in to the University, Buddy?"

"Yep, all set, Mom, classes start mid-September. All set."

Mid-September, I thought. Buddy's school didn't start until mid-September. But he was going to college, not grade school. School would start here the end of August, just before the jump.

If the grade schools here and in Seattle had a schedule like the university it would be no problem. I could go to the jump, then start school in Seattle. But this darn school schedule was a problem, and I still hadn't said anything to my mom.

When she called on Sunday, I told her I'd made lots of friends, that I was tired of moving. I heard nothing but silence on the other end of the line.

I couldn't believe what I told her next. "I'd like to go to school here." I figured after the jump I'd tell her I wanted to come to Seattle, and she'd be so happy she wouldn't even ask any questions.

"It's different this time, Pick," Mom said. "I've had this job for almost two months now, and I'm doing good. Got a nice place." She paused, and then as if she was offering this as enticement, she said, "I've met someone, Pick. A nice man and he has a boy just a bit older than you."

Now it was time for silence on my end. Finally I said, "Well, I guess you don't need me anymore then, do you?"

Mom said nothing and I felt like I might as well have hit her in the face, my words were so harsh and stunning, and mean.

Finally she said, "We'll talk about this more next Sunday." Her voice sounded more firm, more confident than usual, and I just said, "Okay."

One day, the middle of August, as Buddy, Grandma Grace, and I sat for dinner, Buddy said. "They got the government permit yesterday to land on the north side."

He'd told us earlier that the north side was state-owned land and the state was requiring the permit, because the Skycycle 2 was being considered an airplane.

"Yesterday," Grandma Grace asked. "The thirteenth of August. Hope that isn't an omen."

Buddy laughed. "A fellow like Evel can't depend on good luck or bad luck. If he did . . . well, the number of the permit was 1313."

The following Sunday when my mom called she said, "Your Grandma Grace and I have been talking." She paused for a really long time. "My probation will be over after Christmas."

"Probation?" I asked with concern. Had she been in trouble with the law? "Did you do something wrong?"

"Oh, no." She laughed. "Nothing wrong. I'm doing real good at my job. It's how the big corporations are doing it now. To see if you're suited for the job. They give you six months and then you're a real employee with benefits and everything. Vacation pay. Medical insurance."

So, she wasn't a real employee yet? I wondered. Maybe she wouldn't keep this job at all.

She didn't say anything more for a long moment as if she was waiting for me to say something, or maybe just thinking through what she was going to say next. "If you want to stay . . ."

Was she giving me up this easily? I think I felt more hurt, more confused, than happy.

"Start school there first semester, 'til I'm set for sure in the job . . . though I have no doubt," she added. "I'm doing good, Pick, really, I am. After Christmas I'll come get you."

"Well, okay," I said reluctantly. I thought I should feel happy that I would get to stay. But the feelings inside me were confusing, and not at all what I thought I'd feel if I really got my way and got to stay. "Well, okay," I said again.

On August 20th, despite the pleas of his Twin Falls promoter to cancel the event, and much to the relief of Buddy and the others working on the Snake River Canyon jump, Evel successfully jumped thirteen Mack Trucks in Toronto, Canada. No injuries to cause problems with the Idaho event. His test launch of Skycycle 2, four days later in Twin Falls, was not as great a success. It was done early, before sunrise, the press not even alerted.

Buddy told me that it landed in the river.

"So, they have to get it out before he can jump?" I asked.

"This was a test cycle," Buddy explained. "The real Skycycle 2 won't be ready until after the tests."

I knew they were building the Skycycles in California, not Idaho, but it sounded like the Skycycle 2—the one Evel would ride across the canyon—was really Skycycle 3, and it looked like two, the old rusty one on display at the site, as well as the test Skycycle that Buddy had told me was a real tight fit, had both taken off and failed. The odds weren't looking good to me.

"A little trouble with the parachute, but they'll get it worked out," Buddy reassured me. "As Evel said, 'third time's the charm.'"

As the last of August drew near and September approached, we all noticed a change in the air. People were talking like the town was about to be invaded by alien visitors. Some of them had already arrived, staking out their campsites. I heard the talk down at Crowley's.

"Better bring out the guns," one of them said. "The town's going to be invaded by Hell's Angels."

"Not to mention the drug-addled hippies with sacks full of pot and psychedelic drugs."

"That's one thing about Evel," another chimed in. "He's a good man. Good American. Speaks out against any kind of narcotics."

"While he's downing a pint or more of Wild Turkey every night."

"Just trying to drink his confidence," another said with a laugh.

"He's going to chicken out."

"No, he's a man of his word," another said.

"All I can say," the original doomsayer came back in. "Unlock your guns. Lock up your wife and daughters."

"There's been some talk that school will start late, wait until after Labor Day, after the county fair, after the jump."

"That's a bunch of crap," another said.

"School will start right on time, end of August."

All this talk of school made me nervous. If they really waited until after the jump, I could go to Seattle then, wouldn't even have to start here. Part of me was wishing maybe that would happen, but I was pretty sure it wouldn't.

And, just like the men at Crowley's said, school started right on time, the end of August. I went to Bickle Grade School, and both Ricky and Jeff were in my class, so it didn't even feel that strange. I already had friends, and the schoolwork wasn't hard.

School was out for Labor Day, though it seemed like it had just begun. Then when the county fair started, lots of the kids who were in 4-H and were showing animals at the fair skipped days altogether. Grandma Grace said some of them spent the nights right there in the stalls with their animals.

Grandma and Buddy took me to the county fair the second night, Twin Falls Day. We went through barns of sheep and cattle and horses, and then over to the carnival and Buddy took me up in the Ferris wheel and the hammer, while Grandma Grace watched.

The place smelled of hot dogs and caramel apples and popcorn, but Grandma Grace said it wasn't safe to buy food from the carnival vendors; there were plenty of locals selling food that was safe outside the *midway* as she called it.

Throngs of people strolled through the carnival midway, some of them surely not from Twin Falls County, aliens in leathers and bandanas, men with long, untamed whiskers and even tougher walks. Between the carnies manning the games and rides at the carnival, and the tough-looking strangers, it seemed right here in Twin Falls County a new little show of freaks and outcasts had come to share the excitement of these late summer days. The theme of the fair that year was "Hi, Neighbor!" but a lot of these fairgoers looked nothing like our Twin Falls neighbors.

Outside the carnival grounds, we got hot dogs and roasted

corn from local vendors, those Grandma Grace said we could trust. We went to the rodeo where a dozen girls were competing for the crown to be Miss Rodeo Idaho. Pretty local girls raced into the arena on slick, graceful horses, smiling and waving out at the audience with one hand, skillfully holding the reins with the other.

When we left late that night, there were rows of enormous motorcycles, the type we seldom saw in Twin Falls, parked out in the parking lot. I realized that some of these motorcycles belonged to the strangers strutting along the carnival midway as if they intended to take over the county. The invasion was in full swing! Hell's Angels had arrived. I glanced over at Buddy as we left the fairgrounds and I could see a hint of excitement in the set of his jaw.

On the way home, Buddy explained they were not all Hell's Angels. They were fellows from a variety of groups, motorcycle clubs, as he called them.

"Lot of them Viet Nam vets. Served their country. Like your dad," he said, glancing into the back seat where I sat alone. He and Grandma exchanged looks and I sensed she was telling him to shut up.

Later that night when I got into bed, Buddy came in and sat on the edge.

"You want to talk about your dad?" he said.

I nodded and sat up.

"He was a lot of fun. Had a real sense of adventure."

"Is that why he went to war?"

"He loved his country, Pick," Buddy said slowly. "That's why most men go to war."

I didn't know what to say, so I sat still, waiting for Buddy to say more.

"A lot of people don't think what we did in Viet Nam was right. It wasn't like when Grandpa Jack fought in World War II. We'd been invaded then. The Japanese had attacked us in Pearl Harbor. That's in Hawaii. So we were fighting back, protecting our country. It's a little different . . ."

"Then why did we go to war?"

"You know what communism is?"

Again I nodded, though I only had a vague idea.

"If the communists start taking over, even in places far from here . . . well, they just want to keep taking, taking away freedoms. That's what we were fighting for ... freedom. But, the vets coming back . . ." Buddy took in a deep gulp as if considering whether to continue explaining, because it was pretty obvious my dad didn't come back. "They weren't greeted as heroes, like Grandpa Jack when he came home. A lot of these men could see what they'd done over there wasn't appreciated. Some of the fellows felt lost when they came back home, needed to be around others who understood what they'd been through. Some of them found that in motorcycle clubs, being around other vets."

We weren't really talking about my dad, but I wondered if Buddy thought my dad would be in a motorcycle club. Sometimes I did wonder what my dad would be like now, what he'd be doing, what kind of job he'd have.

"Did you want to go to war?" I asked Buddy, then wished I hadn't. Even in the dark room, barely able to see Buddy's face, I sensed I'd asked a hard question.

"I was pretty young when . . . and then, going off to college." Buddy's voice trailed off and then he leaned down and kissed me on the head, like he was my mom. "Lots of things in life that are hard to understand, hard to explain." After a moment he stood. "Night, Pick," he said as he closed the door.

The next evening Buddy didn't make it home for dinner. Grandma Grace sat in her chair in the front room, reading the paper, and I was on the floor, doing some homework. Suddenly she broke out in laughter, which was strange in itself because Grandma Grace wasn't what you'd describe as a laugher, but more of a snorter.

"Why, look at this, Pick." She shook the paper out and handed it to me, pointing.

"Mr. Swensen put out a display in his meat counter, offering a special on baloney, in celebration of the big event that's about to take place, honoring the man hailed as an American hero, a man, who according to Mr. Swensen is full of baloney."

I looked at the ad and sure enough, Swensen's Market was offering a special on baloney. There was no doubt who Mr. Swensen thought was full of it. He stated if Evel Knievel actually made the jump he'd reward him with a twenty-pound baloney.

Friday afternoon before the launch, right after school, before Grandma Grace got home, Ricky came over and asked if I wanted to ride down to City Park. "Hell's Angels are camping out there," he said, talking so fast, so wound up I thought he might explode. "Putting up tents, some throwing sleeping bags out on the bare grass." He whispered, "Smoking weed. Motorcycle gangs, girls too . . ." He was so excited he was actually hiccupping. "Doing it right there!" He didn't say what, but the way he emphasized *it*, I had a pretty good idea. "Out in the open. Next to the bandshell. Over by the kiddy pool."

I thought of the girl I'd seen at the park tending the little kids, reading her book. The girl I'd seen once more at the Harmon Park pool in the red bathing suit, and somehow for some reason I hoped she hadn't seen this. Then I thought of Grandma Grace. She drove right by that park to work every day. But she hadn't said anything, and she hadn't told me I couldn't go to City Park.

"Sure," I said. We went out to the shed and got my bike, then headed down to the park.

I'd spent a lot of time at City Park that summer, sometimes just zipping through on bikes with my friends, or playing on the lava rocks. It wasn't as big or as busy as Harmon Park with the pool and baseball diamonds that kept the place pretty active all summer. The big event at City Park was the weekly band concert held every Thursday night. The city band performed, playing in the bandshell that looked like an enormous concrete seashell. Grandma Grace and I always walked over, sometimes Buddy went, too. Old people with canes and lapdogs sat on the wooden benches lined up in a row like an outdoor theater. Families lounged on blankets spread out on the grass, while little kids danced to the music, and couples, both old and young, snuggled and swayed, many slurping ice cream or snacking on popcorn. The public library stood on one side of the park, and on the opposite side, a junior high and courthouse. A number of churches skirted the periphery, along with a two-story brick building, the town's one Catholic grade school. It was a friendly, relatively quiet, family park.

But when Ricky and I arrived at City Park, it was barely recognizable. Tattooed, burly, hairy, pony-tailed, barrel-chested, black leather-clad men prowled the park, amidst canvas tents. Enormous, powerful Harleys, snorting out smoke and thunder, cruised defiantly down the small walking lane that vertically bisected the small park. No one paid any attention to the *no motor vehicles allowed* signs. A machine, the likes of which I had never seen, a hybrid contraption, part VW bus, part motorcycle, instantly caught my eye. Motorcycle gangsters sat on bikes or lawn chairs, some sprawled out on the trampled down grass, swigging beers, smoking cigarettes, big old cigars, and hand-rolled sticks that I was pretty sure were neither. With smoke and noise, and loud rock music playing from radios, it was as if we'd slipped into another world. I'd never seen anything so scary and exciting in my entire life.

A makeshift parade of sorts, comprised of snorting, coughing motorcycles, and other improvised vehicles, wheeling and roaring, made its way down Shoshone Street on the west side of the park right in front of the courthouse. A big flatbed truck with more Hell's Angels and girls in bellbottom jeans, leather chaps, and skimpy halter tops moved along the street.

Many held handwritten signs of protest.

Some read: NO TO HELMET LAWS. Others declared:

HELMETS TAKE AWAY OUR PERSONAL RIGHTS.

As cool as Buddy was, he always wore a helmet, and he'd told me that Evel Knievel always wore a helmet, and told kids to wear helmets, even while riding bikes—though I'd never in my life seen a kid on a bike wearing a helmet. And Evel always warned kids to stay away from narcotics.

Well, the way these Hell's Angels were carrying on, jumping around on their bikes, hair flying freely, I had a pretty good idea they were using narcotics. Not a single one was wearing a helmet.

"Look at that," Ricky squealed. "That girl's taking off her shirt!"

I looked over at the flatbed truck, and sure enough, one of the girls was taking off her top, then holding up her tits with her hands, as if to show off what she had. Then one of the Hell's Angels, a guy in a leather jacket with a bunch of patches on both the front and back, hollered, "Show us your titties," to another girl, who laughed and took another chug of her beer. But before we knew it that flatbed truck was strewn with beautiful, shirtless girls, showing their titties exactly as instructed.

Ricky and I were so enthralled, engrossed and rapt at this other-worldly scene playing out right before our eyes, that we didn't even notice the police officer, who was most likely just peacefully supervising what really wasn't a riot—they were protesting peacefully—who walked up behind us.

"You boys have permission to be here?"

Something inside me jumped, not a good thing as my insides were already behaving strangely. I glanced back, taking a deep gulp of air. I was thinking maybe he was going to haul us in, that we were in big trouble. But then I realized we had done nothing wrong. We were in a city park, surrounded by churches and schools, and a library and courthouse, a park I'd been to lots of times before, a park my Grandma Grace drove past every day when she went to work. (Again, I wondered if Grandma Grace had seen any of this, but I knew, of course she had.)

"You boys need to get on home," the policeman said in a

deep voice, which left no doubt he was a man of authority. "This is no place for a couple young boys."

This is a city park. This is our park, I thought, but both Ricky and I hopped back on our bikes. On the way home, I glanced over several times, and Ricky's expression was an exact reflection of mine, excitement mixed with disbelief. I raised my arms in the air, then got up some good speed and stood on the seat of my new bike, letting off a super loud holler, looking over at Ricky whose grin was as wide and ridiculous and as joyful as mine.

The night before the jump, Saturday night, I waited up for Buddy. Grandma said with all the commotion in town, all the extra people, Buddy would probably be out late, maybe would even have to stay at the site all night. He'd told us that Evel had flown back to Butte. He wanted to be with his family at home, and he was also throwing a party, a million-dollar party for his friends in Butte, to celebrate what was coming up on Sunday, September 8.

When Grandma Grace sent me to bed, I tossed and turned with excitement, listening for Buddy to come in. When I finally got to sleep, it seemed in a second I was awake again. It was still dark, but I could hear voices in the kitchen and I could smell fresh brewed coffee. I got up, slipped on my pajama bottoms, left my room and started toward the kitchen, but when I could make out the voices of Buddy and Grandma Grace enough to understand what they were saying, I stopped in the hallway.

"I know he thinks I'm going to take him, and in all honesty I was planning on doing it. I know, I know," Buddy said, "You've never thought it's a good idea, but Evel's kids'll be there, Kelly, Robbie, and Tracey, and Bob Arum's got two boys about Pick's age, and he's been waiting all summer." Buddy was quiet then, but I could hear the sound of his coffee cup hitting the table.

"That's the reason he didn't want to go start school in Seattle," Grandma Grace said. "Isn't it?"

Grandma paused for an answer, but if Buddy said anything I

couldn't hear it.

She went on, "I explained to his mom, said he'd be coming along as soon as the jump was over. You know, as much as I despise the man, what he's been stirring up here in the community, I've been praying, praying that he makes it. Especially if Pick was there. Don't want any kid, especially sweet Pick, seeing a man jump to his death." There was another long pause in the conversation, and then I heard footsteps in the kitchen and now imagined Grandma Grace getting up to refill the coffee. "Want a refill?" she asked. "Probably better grab a bite to eat too."

"I'll get some cereal." I heard Buddy push his chair back, and then footsteps to the pantry.

After a few moments, Grandma Grace said, "Maybe it's just all for Pick. I don't know that he would have made it through the summer without Evel Knievel, as much as I hate to say, but . . . not sure you would have made it either, Buddy." Grandma laughed, but it wasn't the laugh like she'd laughed when she read about Mr. Swensen's offer of free baloney. It was a sad, serious laugh.

"I can't take him," Buddy said quietly. "If you think Evel—with all his drinking, carrying on with other women—is bad for a kid, well, that site out there this morning . . . drinking, drugs, crazy wild people that have nothing better in life to do than watch a man jump over a canyon in Idaho. They burned down half the Porta Potties, ripped the top right off a beer truck. This is far from the family affair Evel and his big-time promoters were trying to convince us it is. I wouldn't take a kid down there, and honestly I don't know how Evel can even consider having his own kids there. Most of the local people hired as guards have bailed. Not worth getting beat up, maybe even thrown over the canyon or losing your life over. Don Branker, the fellow brought in by ABC—"

"That long-haired rock-show promoter?"

"Actually a decent fellow. Lot smarter than Evel, that's for sure. Well, he went down to Shoshone Falls where a bunch of the motorcycle gangs are camping out . . ." I noticed Buddy wasn't calling them motorcycle clubs anymore. "Branker promised to pay them $1,000 each, all the beer they could drink to come over to the site and act as guards."

"So the site's now being guarded by Hell's Angels offered a bottomless keg of beer?"

"Looks like that's so. Most of those originally hired have skipped out. Not enough money in Evel's golden pouch to make them risk their lives."

"You're not headed back are you, Buddy?" I could hear the concern in Grandma Grace's voice.

"You know, the fool that he is, that goddamned, stupid ass man, he says he's a man of his word."

"Stupid as all get out," Grandma Grace said, and in her voice, I could see her shaking her head, but there was something else, a mixture of fear and anger.

"I've got to tell Pick," Buddy said. "I've got to tell him he can't go. I'm not risking that kid. No, he can't go. I don't know how to tell him." He was quiet for a long moment. "Should never have set him up for this in the first place. But I've got to go back. Should I go wake him?"

"He'll be getting up soon enough," Grandma Grace said. "He was so darned excited last night, took him forever to get to sleep. I went in late to check on him . . . You go back to work, Buddy," she said, her voice shaking but resigned. "You go back. I'll tell Pick he can't go. He's used to me being a grouchy old woman. Better coming from me. I'll try to explain you're just protecting him. Go now. You got a job protecting that bird-brained man. Doesn't seem he has sense enough to protect himself."

I waited for a few moments, then tiptoed back to my room, pulled on my jeans, my dirty socks from the day before, my shirt, my shoes. I listened until I heard Buddy's motorcycle leaving through the alley, then as quietly as possible I opened the window, pushed out the screen, and crawled out. I hit the grass which was damp with dew. Though the September weather still carried a heavy trace of the summer heat, mornings were brisk, if not downright cold, and I thought of the night we'd slept out in the tent in Ricky's backyard.

Shivering, thinking maybe I should go back for a jacket, then deciding no, I glanced around, and seeing no one, I sneaked into the shed, got out my new bike, then hopped on, pedaled down the alley and headed toward City Park. As I pumped faster and faster the sky had taken on a pink tint as the sun worked its way into the day. Red sky at night, sailor's delight. Red sky in the morning, a sailor's warning. Something Mom used to say, though the sky was more pink than red.

When I arrived at City Park it was early enough that most of the motorcycle gangs were still sleeping. A few of them sat on lawn chairs, warming themselves around an old oil barrel, smoke spiraling up from inside. I was pretty sure a fire in the park was illegal. They were drinking beer and they looked so tired and groggy I thought maybe they had never even gone to bed, that they'd been sitting all night, drinking beer. A girl, who looked barely older than a teenager, stepped out of one of the tents and yawned. She was wearing a bra and cut-off jeans, but she wasn't even shivering. She looked over at me.

"Going to the jump today?" she asked, real friendly.

"My Uncle Buddy's taking me," I lied. "He's Evel Knievel's personal guard."

"A fellow jumped off the canyon yesterday," one of the beer-drinking Hell's Angels said to no one in particular.

A burly man walked out of the tent, put his arm around the girl. "Down at Shoshone Falls. Must have been stoned out of his head. Hopped on his bike—jumped right into the falls. Surprised it didn't kill him."

"Wouldn't that ruin the show," another fellow chimed in. "Evel Knievel's jump to his death upstaged. Now that's supposed to be the show. Don't want anyone else to take away his glory. This is Evel's jump to the death."

74

"Someone's painted a big bullseye target on the north side," the Hell's Angel with the girl said.

They all laughed.

"Think Evel will hit it?"

"Crash right into the canyon wall." One of the men sitting by the barrel punched his fist into his beefy palm and laughed.

"He's going to chicken out," one of the others said.

"No he's not," I said defiantly and they all turned and stared at me. "Evel Knievel is the greatest motorcycle rider of all time and he's going to jump over the Snake River Canyon." But even as I said it I wondered if Evel, too, was going to let me down. Just as Buddy had, just as my dead dad and my mom with her new boyfriend and kid had let me down.

Before any of the Hell's Angels could add more to the conversation, I jumped on my bike and took off as fast as I could. I rode over to Harmon Park pool, sat on the bench in the spectators' area, watching nothing. It was Sunday morning, the clear blue water as still and smooth and silent as an ice skating rink at midnight. I got back on my bike and thought for a moment I'd just ride out there to the site, crash the gate, go in and wait, wait for Evel Knievel to arrive. But I knew they wouldn't let me in. I didn't have a ticket. I had never had a ticket.

I started back home, but then kept pedaling, over one more street, over to Ricky's house, up to his front door where I stopped for a moment. Then I rode right through his front yard, unlatched the gate into his backyard, then out to the garage. I hopped off my bike and stomped into the unlocked garage and stared down at the pieces to the ramp. I lugged them out into the alley. No one was stirring in the neighborhood, some of the early wakers maybe getting ready to take off for the first church services of the morning. I wondered if Grandma Grace was looking for me now, if she'd discovered I was gone. She'd never come looking in the alley. I assembled the ramp. Then as quietly as possible I rolled the garbage cans into the middle of the alley, though such an attempt at silence was impossible. Some of them had garbage in them now, so I kept the lids on tight and rolled. I lined them up. Six. No, I'd do seven. Maybe seven was impossible, but with my new bike, the bike Buddy and Grandma had bought for me, the bike I promised Buddy, the liar, I'd never use to jump garbage cans, I knew I could do it. Even with the old bike, Buddy's hand-me-down, I was better than Greg by a long shot, better than Jeff, even better than Ricky. With this new bike I knew I could do it. I could clear seven with room to spare.

Just as I placed the seventh can, I looked over. Ricky stood staring through the slats in his backyard fence. He was dressed in his church clothes. I could hear his mom calling. I went down to the end of the alley. I started up. By then, his mom was at the fence. Then Buddy and Grandma, coming out from our backyard. And Jeff, and Greg. And I was going faster and faster and faster, hitting the launch ramp with perfection.

Flying. Flying. Flying. Higher than ever. Over one. Two. Three. I was going so fast, and yet everything had slowed down. As I looked out I saw blue sky, then a line of ever-growing spectators. The girl in the red bathing suit was smiling, waving. And my mom was there and someone with a camera. And I knew now, I knew why he did it. I knew why Evel jumped. Because it was the most frightening, most exhilarating feeling in the world and everyone, everyone was watching me and cheering me on.

I cleared the final seventh can, touching with perfection on the landing ramp. Solid. So fast and graceful. Perfect. And then I saw it—Mrs. Fontinelli's big old car, the car she drove only once a week on Sunday to church, backing out of her garage as I slid down the alley, attempting to brake, she glancing over with horror, unable to stop what was about to happen. Then everything went black.

I was in and out of reality for the next few days, reliving the jump in what wasn't really a dream, but a level or two deeper than a dream. My mom, Grandma Grace, and Uncle Buddy, along with a priest, hovered over me. I wasn't sure what was real, what I'd imagined, what had been induced by whatever it was the tubes and clear plastic lines were pumping into my broken body.

When I finally woke enough to know I was in the hospital—that this part was real—I asked, "What time is it?" I didn't really understand why I was there. It had all been a dream. Hadn't it? Yet, here I was.

My mother smiled, her eyes moist with tears, and Grandma Grace tightened her grip on my mother's shoulder and let out a breath of relief that made me think she'd been holding it for more than a second or two.

"It's four o'clock," Uncle Buddy said, glancing at his watch.

"Did he make it?"

"No," Buddy answered. "But, Pick, that was three days ago. It's Wednesday. You've been out for a while. We thought maybe . . ." He couldn't finish.

My mom sat down on the bed next to me, kissed my forehead real careful-like, around all the tubes and wires.

"He's dead?"

"No, just roughed up a bit," Uncle Buddy said. "The chute went off before he even cleared the launch pad."

Later that afternoon, Mom and Grandma went out to get us some burgers, and Buddy stayed, though Grandma Grace said the doctors wouldn't let me eat burgers. I think Buddy was supposed to give me a man-to-man, something neither my mom nor grandma could do. I think he was supposed to tell me how stupid I'd been and how I'd scared Mom and Grandma to death. But instead of giving me a lecture, Buddy described in detail what had happened, not to me, but to Evel.

"He comes out of his trailer dressed to go, struts up to the launch pad, smiling and waving to the crowd. But you can tell he's scared. He's wearing a red-white-and-blue jumpsuit, not his regular leathers. The sun beats down, 90 degrees, and he'd have been drowning in sweat in those leathers. They have a priest, some fellow from Montana, says a benediction, and then David

Frost, the guy they'd hired to host the closed-circuit, climbs up there right in Evel's face, and even from where I stand, I can see the sweat pouring off Evel's brow. That man's scared, scared silly, but he knows he's promised to do it, and I'm pretty sure he figures he's going to die. Made him . . ." Buddy cleared his throat before going on. "Made him pretty grumpy over those last few days. A guy figures he's walking right toward his own death, you'd figure he'd start treating people nice, preparing to meet his Maker. But with Evel, just seems the opposite. That last news conference, well, he came out of the trailer to meet the press, and he plopped down on the trailer stairs as if he were too tired to face them eye to eye. This NBC cameraman, this short little fellow that couldn't have been much taller than you"—Buddy placed his hand out at a bit over my height—"Well this little guy, this cameraman asked Evel if he wouldn't mind standing so the news people could get some shots. He didn't say it rude or demanding, just a simple request, and Evel, well he lets loose cussing and swearing and says, 'I'm not standing for no one.' Well he didn't. Not right away. When he finally got up, he stomped back into his trailer. Later he came back out all full of apologies, and he caught the little man's eye and said, "Why don't you smile,' and this fellow—"

"The NBC cameraman?"

Buddy nodded. "He says to Evel, 'I don't smile for anyone.' Then Evel takes off through the crowd. His cane swinging, slapping at the little fellow, who's still holding his camera, one of those big expensive TV cameras, and Evel whacks him so hard, he falls over, and the camera, well, when Evel's finished with that it doesn't look too good."

"Was he okay, the cameraman?"

"Shook up a bit."

"So, the day of the launch, Sunday?" I asked, wanting to get back to what we'd all been waiting for.

"After the prayer, the interview, Evel hops into the cage-like chair. They hoist him up to the rocket, dangling from a crane.

Though he could have walked up there, that isn't his style. He's waving as they hoist him up."

A show. I thought of Grandma Grace's words.

"The loudspeakers are playing a song, 'Ballad of Evel Knievel,' as he's lifted up. Then Evel's own voice, prerecorded, reading a poem, about doing his best." Buddy shook his head. "It's 3:36 in the afternoon and we all know then that he's not going to chicken out, but at least half the people there are thinking he's facing his last launch. He's going to die."

"But you said he didn't."

"No. The man's still alive, but leaving behind a lot . . ." Buddy paused. "I couldn't have taken you, Pick. That place was a mess after Saturday night, and the people out there at the site, not the nice people you're used to here in Twin Falls. Bad people, using drugs, doing things a kid shouldn't see."

I knew Buddy wasn't going to tell me what they were doing, but I guessed there were things like Ricky and I saw at City Park, only worse. I remembered what he'd told Grandma Grace about the burned Porta Potties and beer trucks.

"But the rocket launched?" I asked.

"Evel's in the rocket now, helmet on, still sweating, stuck in that tight little Skycycle, no getting out now. All he has to do is press the button, and he's off." Buddy stopped again, looking down at me. "You know, Pick, I didn't know about your accident. I wouldn't have gone out there to the launch if I'd known. Your grandma and Ricky's mom took you to the hospital, tried to figure out how to let me know. But by then I was out at the site, no way to get in touch with me."

"So, he pushes the button," I urged him on. "And then . . ."

"Nobody knows for sure what exactly happened. And I don't know if we'll ever know. The rocket launched sure enough, but before he even cleared that launch pad, the drogue chute released. The Skycycle might have had a chance of making it over, but the winds, well you know how the wind blows out on that canyon edge, and it was going strong, about 20 m.p.h., and slapped that rocket right back toward the south side.

"So he made it out? He got out?"

"Well, Evel's still inside the rocket, and the chute's out, and with the wind, that Skycycle rocket rolls and flips down, down, down into the canyon."

"The river? He ends up in the river?"

"From the south side, we can't really see . . . and that's where all hell breaks loose. You know the fences? The fence Evel refused to have cemented into the ground because the price was too high? And the fence built around the launch pad and press area?"

I nodded, but didn't say a word.

"Well, those crazy druggies, boozers, gangs, hippy-dippy nudies, idiots, well, they figure they've paid their twenty-five bucks, and now they can't see a darned thing. They paid good money and this is the show they get? Two seconds and the rocket takes a vertical dive down. If you'd blinked you would have missed it. So they start rushing toward the canyon edge, at least ten thousand strong, taking out one fence and then the other, hanging there, pushing, shoving trying to get a better look."

"Did anyone go over? Get killed?"

"Amazingly, no. I hear one girl got pushed over, caught on some rocks, probably so boozed up she just bounced. No. No one was killed, or even seriously injured. People would hate to admit it, but those Hell's Angels, the ones Branker picked up down at Shoshone Falls, they stood their ground, kept a lot of the crowd back, probably saved lives that day."

"Did he land in the river?"

"Everyone thought he was dead. But we couldn't see. Couldn't see a darned thing." Buddy took in a deep breath, then exhaled as if he were reliving it now. "A helicopter hovered overhead. A small rowboat, with some of the crew who'd been hired to look after things, was situated down in the canyon. In case the Skycycle and Evel needed to be pulled up. Heck if I know how that was supposed to work. Little rowboat pulling out all that metal. But the rocket didn't land in the river at all. With that chute out, the strong headwind, the Skycycle came right back toward the south side, bounced into the canyon wall, ricocheted, fell about fifty feet, then bounced down to within a few feet of the Snake."

I could picture the piles of lava rock along the river at the base of the canyon.

"Evel's still in the cockpit," Buddy continued. "I don't know what would have happened if he'd been successful in getting out. Probably would have gone right into the river. Drowned. Two of the men on the rowboat reach him. One fellow, I think you might have met him on the site, named John, came down on a rope from the helicopter, got to Evel, helped him out, got him into the boat, then transferred Evel to the helicopter. Wasn't long and they brought him back to the launch site."

"Evel?"

Buddy nodded. "Boy, people were mad, mad as all get out. Paid twenty-five bucks to see that half-assed attempt. People were mad, but Evel . . . roughed up a bit, scratches all over his face. Maybe that made people all the madder thinking they got ripped off and all Evel has is a few scratches on his face."

"All scratched up from the lava rocks in the canyon?"

"More likely self-inflicted, scratching himself on the face, going nuts trying to get that flight helmet off, not even realizing it was still locked. Think he went a little crazy."

"What happened? Why did the chute go off? Would he have made it if it hadn't?"

"Don't know that we'll ever know the answers to those questions. Some are saying he panicked, hit that chute deploy button as soon as it launched. Others say a malfunction that he couldn't have controlled." Buddy shook his head. "They didn't even bother to go back down into the canyon to get John. Poor fellow had to climb up himself. Spent the night down in the canyon. Come Monday morning, when he grabbed the last lava outcrop, pulled himself up onto the rim, he says it looked like all hell had broke loose on the south side. If the destruction the day before the launch took place was bad, well, you couldn't believe that site come Monday morning. A war zone, like bombs dropped, incinerating everything left—the remaining Porta Potties, vendor trucks, concession stands—a mess. Fires still smoldering."

We were both quiet for a moment, and then Buddy said, "I couldn't take you, Pick. I'm sorry." He looked down at me. And I could tell he was—sorry. Maybe even thinking it was his fault that I was here in the hospital.

"Is that why you jumped?" he asked.

I thought for a moment, then said, "I don't know." And I really didn't. I knew it had something to do with me being mad, but I didn't really understand why I'd done it.

"You know, Pick . . ." He glanced around the room. "When I first met Evel, I thought he was one of the most interesting people I'd ever met. Charismatic. Do you know what that means?"

I wasn't sure, but Buddy didn't give me time to answer.

"He's the type of person who could walk into a room and he'd be the center of attention. He'd start telling a story and everyone would listen. And he didn't seem to care what people thought. Just do as he pleased. I guess maybe that was the initial attraction. I was in a personal state of mind myself where I liked that, knowing a fellow who could do whatever he pleased and not really give a . . ." Buddy searched for the right word.

"Damn?" I offered.

Buddy laughed. "Sometimes, well, maybe every one of us finds ourselves in that way . . . not really wanting to care what anyone thinks. It's not a good place to be, Pick. Because if you don't care what people think, you don't much care about anything. And sometimes you do things that can hurt yourself and others too. And, you know, the more I got to know the man, well his stories just didn't add up. He'd tell it one way, one day, tell it a completely different way the next. Maybe to make himself look better, or tougher, or . . . but it got to a point where you couldn't believe what the man told you. And he did things to hurt people."

"Like the TV cameraman?"

Buddy nodded. "But, maybe even worse, people he loved. He's got a nice wife. Nice family. Sometimes he'd be here in town, family left back in Butte." Buddy stopped, as if considering if he should go on. "Not acting like a married man at all."

I had a pretty good idea what he meant, but Buddy didn't go into any more detail on that topic.

"You know, Pick, maybe I shouldn't have told you I'd take you to the launch. But maybe I just wanted you to have something really special this summer."

I thought about what Grandma said early the morning of the jump, when she and Buddy were talking in the kitchen, how she said she didn't think I would have made it through the summer, how maybe Buddy wouldn't have either if it hadn't been for Evel Knievel and the Snake River Canyon.

"You know, Pick, Evel's just a showman. Risking his life to put on a show. Maybe for the money, but I think even more than that, for the attention."

Was Buddy telling me I was like Evel, that I just wanted attention?

"That's not a real hero. The real heroes are fellows like your dad, serving his country, giving his life for his country. People like your mom, working hard, doing her best to take care of you. Leaving you here, even though it wasn't what she wanted, to set up a new and better life for you both in Seattle. Get a good job, a place to live."

I nodded.

"People like Grandma Grace, those are the real heroes."

"Grandma Grace?"

"People who work hard, take care of their families, then go

the extra mile to do something nice for someone else."

"Like taking the quilts to the kids in the hospital?"

"Exactly," he said, and I could hear Mom and Grandma Grace coming down the hall, and I could smell the Arctic Circle hamburgers and fries with special sauce in the paper bags they carried into my room that day.

I stayed in the hospital five more days. Mrs. Fontinelli, who felt terrible about what had happened in the alley that day, though everyone knew it was my fault, not hers, came to visit every day. Being the retired school teacher she was, she brought in my homework to help me so I wouldn't fall behind in my schoolwork.

They even let Ricky, and Jeff, and Greg in to see me. They wanted to know all about my jump over seven garbage cans, and it was then that I knew I'd dreamed most of it. Ricky wasn't there, didn't even know 'til after Grandma Grace came over to ask his mom to drive so they could get me to the hospital. And I knew the other stuff, like the girl in the red bathing suit, well, she wasn't there either. But, I had jumped those seven garbage cans and if it hadn't been Sunday morning, if Mrs. Fontinelli hadn't been pulling out of her garage to go to church at that very moment . . .

Buddy and I watched the launch and Evel Knievel interviews on TV. It was a lie, the part about the only people who'd see it were those who paid for the closed-circuit TV. The week after it played on TV I took off with my mom for Seattle.

I've lived there for almost forty years now, working as an engineer for Boeing for the past twenty-eight. When I got to Seattle when people asked, I said my name was Mike. I'd left Pick behind in Idaho.

~~~

Grandma Grace passed away at the age of ninety-two. She lived in her house alone, doing fine until the last few days, and Buddy was close by to help out. He's lived there since he graduated from University of Idaho a couple of years after I spent the summer. He married, a pretty Twin Falls girl, and had a couple of kids, my cousins, much younger than me. They've got kids now too, and so do I.

My wife and I have come for Grandma Grace's funeral, and are now headed home. My mom and her husband, my step-dad, are staying some extra time to help Buddy and his wife get the house ready to sell. My step-brother, and my two boys, flew in, but had to get back to jobs in Washington state.

Driving out of town with my wife, we stop at the viewing area in front of the visitors' center along the rim of the canyon, though the center has been closed down since the end of summer. It is late fall, a few months past the time of year when Evel Knievel attempted to jump the Snake River Canyon.

A new Perrine Bridge, the one they were working on the summer Evel attempted his jump, now spans the canyon, and a walking path winds along the upper edge. Shopping centers, offices, and restaurants have sprouted up along the canyon rim, a sure sign of the city's growth and development over the years.

The view is still fantastic. That hasn't changed at all. From the path, as it dips beneath the bridge, you can still see the ramp, looking a little worn down, but still visible from the distance. There's talk that, for the fortieth anniversary of the Evel Knievel jump, another daredevil is going to attempt to jump the Snake River Canyon from the same spot.

There's something about this town that still carries a hint of innocence, yet it's doubled in population and businesses like the Greek yogurt plant and a company that makes energy bars for outdoor enthusiasts have found homes for their factories, providing hundreds of jobs and bringing new people into the valley.

Some of the old part of town where Grandma Grace lived appears a bit neglected, though her small home, with Buddy's help, was always kept in good repair. I took a walk through the old neighborhood, noticing the weeds in Mrs. Fontinelli's garden, thinking of all the pennies I could have earned by pulling them up. She's been gone for years. The Edsens' garage is looking pretty shabby, too, flaking paint, missing shingles. Ricky's parents are still in town but moved into one of the new subdivisions. I saw Mrs. Edsen at the funeral and she told me Ricky is in Montana, working as a foreman for a big construction company.

As my wife and I walk along the path on the south side of the canyon, we notice a group of young men. Base jumpers getting ready to jump right off the bridge. It's legal here and attracts the adventurers.

I hear a young couple talking, pointing.

"That's where Evel Knievel jumped the canyon?"

A man, wearing sweats, walking, pumping arms and legs, slows, then stops. He is about my age, maybe a few years older.

"You know he didn't make it?" he tells the young couple. "Went straight down." He points.

"You saw it?" they ask.

"I was sitting on the roof at a friend's house along the canyon." Again he gestures. "Watched him go up, then right straight down." He makes a motion with his hand, like it's the rocket. "We all thought he was a goner."

"But he survived?"

The man nods. "Some view it as the biggest failure of all times around here. But put us on the map, that's for sure." He gazes off, down toward the falls before adding, "You know what else happened that day, the day Evel Knievel launched himself over the Snake River Canyon? Not many around here remember."

I know, but I want the man to tell them.

"Ol' Evel Knievel got knocked right off the top headlines on the front pages of newspapers all over the world. The day before the jump, President Ford pardoned President Nixon for his part in the Watergate affair."

I'm not sure the young couple has any idea of this history.

"All the hoop-a-la here in Twin Falls," the man continues, but the young couple's eyes are set on the group of base jumpers who have just launched off the bridge. It is a sight to see as they glide gracefully down toward the winding Snake River against the backdrop of a perfect blue sky, their colorful rainbow chutes opening, outlined by dark stone, finally landing on the floor of the canyon.

The man goes on, talking to no one in particular, then turns toward me and my wife. "I guess some still haven't forgiven Evel for the mess he made here in town. Left unpaid bills, food vendors going broke. His fans torched a good chunk of land and property. Yeah, some haven't forgiven him, but you know what?" His voice goes low, almost a whisper, and he's now directing this toward me. "That summer was the best time I've ever had." He laughs and takes off along the path.

I smile at my wife, but say nothing. She knows about my summer in Twin Falls, the summer of Evel Knievel, even about the girl in the red bathing suit, and my crash in the alley. Yet, I've never told her it was the best summer of my life.

Readers Guide

EVEL KNIEVEL JUMPS
THE SNAKE RIVER CANYON

READERS GUIDE

QUESTIONS FOR DISCUSSION

1. The story is told from the point of view of a ten-year-old boy. Do you think Pick is a reliable narrator? Why or why not?

2. Pick describes Grandma Grace as being bossy and possessing a let's-get-things- done attitude. Do you believe this is an accurate description? Are there other traits revealed through her interaction with other characters in the story?

3. Pick sees Evel Knievel as a true American hero, not fake like superman, yet Evel appears in the story only through what Buddy tells Pick and through what Pick overhears. Do you believe the real Evel is ever presented in the story?

4. Pick often admits to lying to his grandmother or withholding details about his and Buddy's activities. How much of what Pick does that summer do you think Grandma Grace is aware of? What can you point out in the story that reveals a deeper awareness?

5. When Buddy asks Pick why he jumped, he replies that he doesn't know. Do you believe this is the truth? Why do you think he jumped?

6. When Buddy refers to Evel doing what he does for attention, Pick questions if this is his own true intention. Do you think there are scenes in the story when Pick is trying to get attention?

7. Early in the story Pick sees Twin Falls as a place filled with hicks. Does this change over the course of the summer? How does the big event on September 8 affect the people of Twin Falls and specifically Pick?

8. By the end of the story do you believe Pick's idea of a true hero has changed? Do you think there are any true heroes in the story? Who would you describe as the hero of the story?

9. Are there events in your own childhood that you look back on with a different perspective than you had as a child? Is the town where you grew up anything like Twin Falls, Idaho?

10.How do you interpret the last line of the story?

STORIES

from those who were there

Evel Knievel Jumps the Snake River Canyon . . . and Other Stories Close to Home was published in 2014 to commemorate the 40th anniversary of Evel's jump over the Snake River Canyon and consisted of a novella and short story collection.

In 2022, eight years after the original publication, a couple of years before the 50th anniversary of the jump, I started thinking it might be fun to republish the book on the 50th anniversary in 2024, retain the novella but replace the short stories with true-life recollections of those who were there for the jump.

While writing the 2014 novella, as my characters Pick, Grandma Grace, Uncle Buddy, Ricky, and Danny came to life in my imagination, much of the Twin Falls setting was drawn from my own memories of growing up in a small town in south-central Idaho. But, my personal experience of the Evel Knievel event was limited as I was living in Boise then, just visiting for the weekend to watch the jump that took place on Sunday afternoon, September 8, 1974. I'd talked to family members in Twin Falls, but I hadn't been around for any of the preparations, buildup, or excitement during the summer before Knievel's jump. I had merely come back home to witness this historic event. And I hadn't hung around for the cleanup.

Though I am primarily a fiction writer, I tend to write about actual events and have always attempted to create believable stories. For the original novella, I did my research, reading numerous magazine and newspaper articles, as well as books about Evel Knievel. Some of the accounts about the Twin Falls jump were written by locals for the *Times-News*, the primary newspaper covering the Magic Valley. I visited the Twin Falls Public Library, digging into boxes of microfiche and making copies of local articles. I also read stories and Evel Knievel profiles in national magazines such as *Rolling Stone* and *Sports Illustrated*. These, I realized, were written by nationally recognized journalists and reporters who popped into town specifically for the jump and had never been part of the community. I also scoured the internet for films and stories about Evel Knievel, a man who was already a legend by the time he came to Twin Falls.

For this 50th anniversary publication, I knew I wanted the accounts to be first-hand stories from people who had a real-life connection to Twin Falls rather than outsiders who put in an appearance for the thrill of witnessing an event that was garnering international attention.

So, I set out to find my witnesses. I posted on a Facebook page called "You might be from Twin Falls, Idaho . . ." The post included an image of my original 2014 book cover and a black and white photo of Evel sitting in his Skycycle, ready to launch over the Snake River Canyon. I posed the question, "Where were you on September 8, 1974?" Many responded. Everyone who lived in Twin Falls during the summer of '74, and those, like me, who were relocated Twin Falls natives returning home for the Event of the Century, as many fans called it, knows the answer to this question.

After the Facebook posting, I followed up on responses that looked promising and sent out private messages to these people, but I still wasn't sure this project was a doable idea. After almost 50 years, old memories could prove troublesome. Could I trust these memories? Because of my own schedule and those of prospective witnesses, it would be several weeks before we were able to arrange a time to talk.

In the meantime, a few weeks later, in September 2022, I attended a class reunion in Twin Falls. It was supposed to be our 55th reunion, but because of the Covid Pandemic, it took place 56 years after our graduation. Several classmates asked what I was up to, if I was still writing books. I was at a point in my life where I often felt I was done writing for publication, but revisiting the Evel Knievel story kept nagging at me. It was definitely a conversation starter with these friends who'd grown up in Twin Falls. When I mentioned my idea to fellow classmate and local realtor Lynn Rasmussen, he told me he hadn't been there for the jump, but he thought Steve Swope might be helpful. Steve was standing nearby, and, though I have no recollection of ever talking to Steve during my four years of high school, we struck up a brief conversation, and I asked if he might have some memories he'd be willing to share. Back in the sixties, when we were in school, there was only one high school in town, so everyone went to Twin Falls Senior High School. With over 400 in our class, it wasn't unusual that Steve and I had probably never spoken. We didn't have any classes together, and looking back, I don't think we had much in common. I remembered Steve as a cute boy with a bit of swagger. I was a shy honor society nerd, and Steve was more into motorcycles and baseball. At this reunion, where everyone was relaxed and comfortable after adding 50+ years of life to the sometimes embarrassing and uncomfortable high school experience, I asked for his number. I even made a lame joke about finally getting his phone number after 56 years. I also snagged his email.

Several weeks after the reunion, my husband Jim had a couple of speaking engagements in Twin Falls, a Rotary Club at noon and a presentation that evening. I hadn't planned on traveling from Boise with him but realized this might be a perfect opportunity to talk to Steve and attempt to nudge some memories out of him about his recollection of the summer of '74 when Evel Knievel came to town. So, I emailed and he agreed to meet me at the Barnes and Noble coffee shop a short distance from the Snake River Canyon while Jim went to his Rotary meeting. Appropriately enough, this big box bookstore is just a mile or so from where Evel attempted his jump, part of the commercial buildup along the canyon edge now dotted with restaurants and retail outlets.

I had scheduled my first interview, and I was on my way . . .

STEVE SWOPE

I arrive at the Twin Falls Barnes and Noble shortly before noon, the time **Steve Swope** and I have set for our meeting. Thankfully, I have time to run to the restroom after my two-hour drive from Boise and numerous cups of coffee that morning. When I step back into the bookstore, I spot Steve scanning a bookshelf with interest. I easily recognize him since I'd seen him just a couple of weeks before at the reunion. I say hello, and he turns and tells me that he just ran into Jim in the parking lot on his way to the Rotary lunch. Though it's already October, Steve wears shorts, an outdoorsy vest, and sneakers. His hair is completely white, and he sports a matching goatee. He looks like a man equally comfortable perusing a bookshelf of recently released titles as one participating in outdoor activities. We step over to the Starbucks coffee shop and get a couple of drinks, flavored iced tea for Steve and a Frappuccino for me.

We find a table, sit, and I briefly explain what I'm attempting to do. Steve says he'll be happy to help if he can. In an earlier email, he'd mentioned that he'd be mining fifty-year-old memories. I thought that was a delightfully alliterative way of saying what we were up to here—mining memories.

Since my intention is to speak with real Twin Falls people, I ask about his background. Even before the interview, I was aware that Steve is a native of Twin Falls and spent his childhood here. After high school, he stayed in the community and raised his family here.

Steve's dad, Charles Swope, was born in Chattanooga, Tennessee, one of a large family with seven kids. They relocated to Idaho for the drier climate. They started out in Gooding. Steve's mom, Velate, grew up in Rupert. Her family originally came from the Isle of Man. Steve's folks met in a grocery store in Rupert, eventually making their way to Twin Falls. Charles served in World War II, drafted at the age of 32, and was already married to Velate. They had no children yet, the prospect of war looming large. He fought in the Battle of the Bulge in Belgium and returned to Idaho, where they finally started a family. Like Steve's dad, mine also served in the war, as did most young men in that generation. It doesn't surprise me that we are already finding common ground in our histories.

We share many memories of growing up in Twin Falls as members of big families. Steve has three brothers and a sister who passed away at a young age. I am one of six, three boys and three girls. We talk about our stay-at-home moms, which was more the norm back then, particularly when large families were common. Raising four active boys, Steve confirms that his mom didn't get much me-time. We both had hard-working dads. Steve's father was part owner of the Pepsi Cola bottling company, and my dad and his brothers owned the local meat packing plant. We share memories of lazy, unstructured days when a kid could hop on a bike and ride all over town with friends, our moms not terribly concerned as long as we showed up for dinner. We talk about roller skating at the Radio Rondevue, swimming at Harmon Park, summer nights at the baseball park nearby where we'd hang out with our friends, drinking soda, eating popcorn and peanuts, and cheering on our team, the Magic Valley Cowboys. I'm guessing it's pretty likely that as grade school kids, even attending different elementary schools—Steve at Bickel and Morningside, me at St. Edward's— we crossed paths as we experienced all that a small town in Idaho offered in the fifties and sixties.

Steve tells me his great loves as a kid were baseball and bikes. As we chat, the conversation morphs into how he became acquainted with Evel Knievel, and I realize Steve has come full circle from bicycles as a kid, motorcycles as a teen and young adult, and now back to good old-fashioned bikes that require a bit of pedal power. He and Sandy, his wife of 46 years, still bike, and their travels often include biking trips.

As it turns out, Steve's interest in motorcycles led to his acquaintance with Evel Knievel, or Bobby Knievel, as his friends back in his hometown of Butte, Montana, called him. Steve tells me the thing that drew him to Evel wasn't the daredevil reputation, Evel's famous jumping stunts, or the bravado which set him up as a hero for many American kids, but his and Bobby Knievel's love of motorcycles.

Several years before the Twin Falls event, Evel had attempted to set up a motorcycle jump over—what else?—the Grand Canyon. Unable to obtain the permission necessary from the federal government, the U. S. Department of the Interior denying him airspace, Evel set his eyes on the Snake River Canyon. It is said that on a flight back to Butte from another event, the deep chasm of the canyon caught his eye, and Evel decided if he couldn't get the Grand Canyon, then the Snake River Canyon just north of the community of Twin Falls, Idaho, would do just fine.

Evel started slipping into town occasionally to get things set up for a jump initially planned for a couple of years earlier than it actually took place. As early as 1970, Evel was telling reporters and anyone who would listen that he would jump the canyon on Labor Day, 1971. Eventually, he threw out another date, July 4, 1972. If there's one thing that went along with the superhero persona that Evel was attempting to project, it was good old American patriotism. So, a July 4th date was perfect, even though the jump was pushed a couple of years forward and didn't occur until late summer of 1974.

But, first, if he was to accomplish this Snake River jump, Evel would need some land for the launch. He began a search. Eventually, he found the perfect spot on the south side of the canyon, just a few miles north of Twin Falls. The property was owned by the Qualls family and used for farming and grazing. Evel told reporters that he bought the land, but it is well known in the community that the Qualls would never sell the land to Evel. But they did agree to lease it for a number of years, about 300 acres, according to Steve, and they were paid a fee of around $30,000.

To win the favor of the Twin Falls community, Evel began to set up a motocross track on the property leased from the Qualls. This is where Steve Swope comes into the picture. I ask Steve exactly what a motocross race is, and he explains that it is a dirt bike race over natural terrain. During this time when Evel was courting the people of Twin Falls, attempting to show them he was serious, that he wanted to do something that would benefit the community, Knievel realized that a well-planned motocross track would bring some attention to the town and pull in some big-name professional motocross racers. Evel began recruiting local fellows to help him build the track. He wasn't paying in anything other than beer, as Steve recalls well, but as Twin Falls merchants and contractors would later learn, Evel didn't always pay his bills anyway. But Steve wasn't being hoodwinked by Evel; he jumped into the project willingly because he was a big fan of motocross racing, and he saw that designing and constructing a track and the publicity developing around this future jumping event planned by Evel would bring in the pros, who would never come to Twin Falls without a well-built track and a sizable purse. Steve recalls working in the cold and rain of early spring days in April and May, and a congenial, friendly Bobby Knievel checking in on the guys from time to time. As Steve brings up memories of seeing Evel out at the site where they were building the motocross track, he can't recall any negative feelings about the man. Evel was often described in the press as a charismatic character, and Steve seems to confirm the assessment.

I ask Steve if the Evel-sponsored, big-name motocross races ever came to fruition, and he tells me they did. He refers to an article in the local *Times-News* in the spring of 1972. Later, I dig into the clippings I saved from the research for my original book and find an article dated late October 1971. It reports a Knievel-sponsored motocross race that "drew cyclists from all over the world." Later that afternoon, after talking with Steve, I go to the local Twin Falls Public Library to check out the article he told me about. The story from early May 1972 lists the riders who won the races the Sunday before. They are pros on the motocross circuit, names I wouldn't recognize though I'm guessing Steve certainly would. In the article with the headline "Yamaha racers win top honors," Evel claims he is presenting the "biggest checks in the sport's history." In another article in the same edition of the *Times-News*, Evel announces that he will pay $50,000 in prizes the following year.

Eventually, after finding and securing his Twin Falls site and setting up the motocross track, Evel began a multi-city promotional tour, traveling around the country, advertising that he's going to jump the Snake River Canyon on his motorcycle. He also told his fans about other events. In addition to the motocross races on the canyon rim, there would be spectacular entertainment for the crowds. The famous Wallendas, a tightrope walking act, would perform. Numerous celebrities would attend. Evel mentioned those he's invited, including the Pope, Elvis Presley, Steve McQueen, Dustin Hoffman, and John Wayne.

"What about the motocross races at the time of the jump?" I ask Steve as we continue our discussion at Starbucks. I tell Steve that I read about Evel touting a purse of over $125,000 for races that would take place in September 1974, just before the scheduled Snake River Canyon jump. Steve tells me he has no memory of those races, that he'd only been involved in the earlier ones after he helped build the track. He seems skeptical of those prizes reaching into the stratosphere.

I ask Steve if he ever ran into Evel after that spring and summer he spent with his friends building Evel's motocross track for nothing but free beer. He says he did run into him once at D.J.'s Lounge—now the location of the Wok 'N Grill— a couple of years later, the summer of the jump. Knievel seemed like a different person from a couple of years prior when Steve first met him. As the day drew closer for the big jump, it was evident that Evel was losing some of his arrogance and congeniality. The buildup, the promo tours, and the efforts to publicize the jump event, things he'd always enjoyed, seemed to be draining the man as the time for the jump arrived. Steve sensed there was a change in Evel. It was getting to him—the possibility that he might fail.

Steve tells me that when he saw Evel at D.J.'s lounge, he said hello, addressing Knievel by his childhood name, Bobby. Steve could see from Knievel's reaction that it didn't offend him. "He acknowledged me," Steve recalls, and said, "You helped set up the track." Their conversation was brief, but as Steve retells the story, he seems impressed that Evel did recognize and appreciate those who had helped him.

Later that summer, as the day of the jump drew near, an influx of visitors poured into the small community, thousands expecting to get in on all the excitement. But, the enthusiasm of the townsfolk was beginning to waver. Steve tells me that when this all started—the possibility that Evel Knievel would perform his most daring stunt right here in our little town—many of those in Twin Falls were thrilled about the publicity, if not notoriety, that such an event would bring. It would definitely put our remote little burg on the map, which a number of residents had initially perceived as a good thing. There was also a belief that money would flow into the community. All these visitors would need places to stay and places to eat. They'd be buying memorabilia and Twin Falls and Idaho souvenirs. But, as people who didn't look like us started to appear on city streets and in parks, concerns began to grow. Tough-looking fellows on motorcycles revved up in parking lots and paraded on loud machines through streets. Some of these contraptions didn't even look like motorcycles to local folks. Hippies arriving in bands were openly using drugs, shedding clothes, and camping wherever they wished. There were reports of campers down at the Falls in the canyon, creating havoc and mayhem. Steve tells me he thinks that Paul Corder, the sheriff at the time, might have decided if they could contain the visitors, keep them all in one spot, this might be the best way to handle the influx. Evel, who was known to stray from the truth, and even when he was in the ballpark of the truth, would certainly tend to exaggerate, had, in earlier promotions, told the press that there would be over 200,000 people coming to town. At the time, Twin Falls had a population of about 22,000, so this was a big deal, even if not as big a deal as Evel wanted to make it.

Steve was hearing the stories, too, and became curious. So, one afternoon, on a whim, he decided to ride his motorcycle down to the Falls. For those unfamiliar with the falls on the Snake River Canyon near Twin Falls, the biggest and most impressive is Shoshone Falls, not the "twin" falls that gave the city its name. Steve's girlfriend and future wife, Sandy, was working, but her sister Cheryl was up for the adventure. Steve hopped on the motorcycle, Cheryl along for the ride. As they headed down the twisting, rock and sagebrush-lined grade to the grassy oasis of the Shoshone Falls Park where the hoards were said to be camping, it didn't take Steve long to realize bringing Cheryl along wasn't the greatest idea. Not long past the sharp curve approaching the park, Steve describes the atmosphere as "Bedlam." The park was filled with some hippies, motorcycle outlaws, nudity, obvious drug use. The crowds were loud and crude, shouting obscenities and making vulgar sexual suggestions. Steve tells me the atmosphere was sometimes referred to as Woodstock's Evil Twin. What Steve is describing sounds like Woodstock without the love.

"Cheryl was a beautiful girl, and I felt protective of her, concerned about putting her in a dangerous situation," Steve tells me. This was not a place to bring a pretty girl like Cheryl. "I turned back. We didn't even get off the bike."

I ask Steve if he was there on September 8 for the jump on the canyon's edge, and he says yes. The price was steep for the day, $25. The only other way to witness the event up close, other than pay this exorbitant price for the onsite experience, was to buy a $10 ticket to watch it live on closed-circuit television projected in movie theaters around the world. Though it would, in fact, show on national TV on ABC's "Wide World of Sports" the following weekend, this wasn't announced ahead of time. Evel wanted to rake in as much cash as he could on the day of the event.

I ask Steve if he paid the $25, and he chuckles a little and tells me, "No."

"Did anyone try to stop you or demand you pay?" I ask. Steve tells me it wasn't a problem at all. He and some of his friends just walked over the field and up to a spot on the east side of the ramp.

My mind wanders back to my own experience of the jump. At this same time, I was sitting on the Holiday Inn golf course just off Blue Lakes Boulevard with my mom, my dad, my youngest brother, a sister, her husband, and a future brother-in-law. Oddly the event took place on a Sunday afternoon, although Evel scheduled it later in the day, after 3:00 p.m. To ensure the churchgoers would be able to attend?

I honestly don't know of any Twin Falls residents who bought a ticket. Most watched from a rooftop, a place on the lawn of one of the businesses along Blue Lakes, or any free spot on private land accessible along the canyon. Or, like Steve, they simply walked over.

"So, you saw it up close?" I ask Steve. "You were actually onsite." I know he got a much better view than I from my greater distance.

So, this is how it goes:

Evel arrives by helicopter and goes to his onsite trail. Shortly, he steps out, wearing his signature red, white, and blue leather jumpsuit. He waves to the crowd. He is secured in a bright red, swing-like box hoisted by a large mechanical crane. The Skycycle awaits him. A poem about promises and patriotism blasts over the loudspeaker. The crowd, already riled up, gets even more excited, shouting and chanting.

Steve confirms that he's seeing some of what he'd witnessed on his quick turn-around trip down to the Shoshone Falls Park. He refers to a number of people in the crowd as "outlaw bikers" rather than Hell's Angels, which many of us use almost as if it is the generic term for motorcycle gangs. The drugged hippies are also present, some of them finding clothing too restrictive for this free-for-all event which has turned into more of a spectacle than anything even Evel planned. Evel dons his helmet and secures himself in the Skycycle. As our hero blasts off, the drogue chute opens right away before he's even cleared the ramp.

From my spot on the golf course at the Holiday Inn, I witnessed none of this. I merely saw the rocket—and it was a rocket, not a motorcycle, no matter what Evel told us, going straight up. Then, straight down. Those sitting on the grass of the golf course, as if we had come for a picnic, stood and gasped, though, from our vantage point, we saw nothing now. We all thought Evel was dead.

"Do you think he chickened out?" I ask Steve now, intrigued with what was obviously his up-front seat to the event. "Did Evel pull the cord on the chute himself?"

Steve tells me he didn't think Evel pulled the chute, though many believe he did. Steve says that even the engineers who built the Skycycle said it was their fault, that it wasn't a failure on Evel's part.

"So, what did you think?" I ask Steve, "when the first chute, then the second larger chute deployed, and Evel dropped straight down into the canyon?"

"I thought at first that he hit the rocks on the south side or possibly drowned in the river."

"So, what happened then?"

Steve tells me that some of the spectators started rushing to the canyon's edge. Everyone wanted to gaze down into the deep chasm to see what happened to Evel. Steve and his friends were off to the side enough that they didn't get caught up in the rush, but they couldn't see down into the canyon either. But things were getting crazy. Hundreds pushed toward the canyon's edge, breaking down the fence that had been hastily and poorly constructed to keep the crowd from going off the rim. Photos taken that day will reveal a scary scene of people who appear to be hanging precariously on the canyon's edge, though we will later learn that no one was killed.

Oddly it doesn't take that long for Evel to be rescued from down along the rough lava rocks below, along the south side of the deep canyon where he's landed, the same side from where the Skycycle launched. He definitely didn't make it to the other side. Miraculously, he didn't land in the Snake. A rescue boat waiting in the river got to him right away, and then the helicopter brought him back to the site to greet his fans.

"So, you saw him right after the jump?' I ask Steve. "How close were you?"

"Close enough to see his bloody face, even his stunned expression. He looked scared to death." As we talk about Evel's possible state of mind at the time, I wonder if Evel was too dazed to realize it wasn't a good idea to return to the launch site, if his handlers were possibly putting him in harm's way. To say the crown went wild is an understatement, and Steve certainly confirms this. At this point, they had transformed from a weird crew of movie-like characters there to cheer on their hero or possibly see a death wish fulfilled to an angry mob upset that Evel had not come through for them in either way.

The crowd, many hopped up on adrenaline, alcohol, and

drugs, was intense, frantic, and angry. They had been duped, tricked by their hero. Evel didn't perform as expected. Steve could see this wasn't a good place to be. "It was crazy, and I told my buddies we needed to get out of there. So, we hoofed it back to where we had parked the pickup on Falls Avenue."

After some thought, Steve says, "The press vilified him," and we talk about how this might have been the beginning of the fall of Evel Knievel, though he continued to perform for years after this.

"So, what was it that contributed to this hero worship?" I ask Steve, circling back to the Evel before this failed jump.

He considers the question a bit. "I think we were looking for a hero, so much going on in our country. We were caught up and divided over the war in Vietnam. Our president, Richard Nixon, had just been impeached." Steve reminds me that the next day, the day after Evel's failed jump, the big news broke that our president, Gerald Ford, had pardoned Richard Nixon. A national story stealing the headlines from Evel Knievel and Twin Falls, Idaho.

"One thing about Evel," Steve tells me, "He never backed down, even when he painted himself into a corner." Something he'd certainly done with this Snake River Canyon jump. Many believed that Evel feared he would not survive this attempt. But he'd said he would do it, and he did. And, though his jump was a failure, he hadn't backed down.

Evel was a true showman, an entertainer, so it's not easy to decipher what was real about the man, what was merely an act. He was a performer on a stage, playing to the crowd there to witness a bizarre circus act. And, yes, he was a hero to many little boys who would beg their parents for an Evel Knievel action toy, but was any of this real?

Steve and I talk about the costumes Evel always wore, the red, white, and blue, stars and stripes forever leather jumpsuits. They were nothing but patriotic, and Steve tells me that he thought that part was genuine, Evel's pride in being an

American. Evel was a patriot. And maybe that was enough for this little town of Twin Falls, Idaho, where we both grew up and still love. To believe that Evel Knievel, with all his bluster and bravado, was, if even for a brief moment, a true American hero.

JOHN KILLEN

I first became aware of *John Killen*'s front-row seat at the Evel Knievel jump through my Facebook group page inquiry, though I've known members of the Killen family for over 60 years. John's older sister Peggy was my high school big sister, a program sponsored by the Twin Falls High Girls' League that matched a senior with a sophomore girl (freshmen still attended junior high) to ease the transition. Peggy was pretty, well-liked by classmates, and kind, and I felt fortunate to have her as my big sister. One of the initiation rituals was the little sisters' march across the bridge just north of town, a 1,500-foot stretch over the almost 500-foot-deep Snake River Canyon. On an unannounced summer morning, as the school year approached, the big sister would show up before dawn and rouse her sophomore sister from bed. Then, with enough daylight to be a spectacle, the younger girls were marched across the bridge in their pajamas, an event much too fun to be called hazing. The original bridge was replaced several years later, construction completed in 1976. Drive over the Perrine Bridge today or stand on the walkway and gaze off to the east. The dirt mound from which Evel Knievel launched his Skycycle is clearly visible.

Peggy's little brother John was three years behind me in school, in the same class at St. Edward's Grade School as my twin sisters, Maggie and Mrezzie, and two of our numerous Florence cousins, Hank and Susan.

So, I was delighted and excited when I learned John had covered the Evel Knievel jump as a "nervous and wide-eyed" reporter, as he described himself in his Facebook post.

John and I sent messages back and forth in the fall of 2022, trying to arrange a time for a phone chat. John was taking off on a ten-day bike ride with two of his sisters, Peggy and Bunnie, and then attending a college reunion in Caldwell where he serves on the alumni board. I had several events on my schedule, too. Finally, we were able to arrange a phone date.

Not surprisingly, the first part of our conversation involves talking about Killen family history and catching up on siblings, John's late brother David (Duke), brother Bill, and sisters Rosemary, Cathy, Peggy, and Bunnie. I seem to recall that the Killens moved to Twin Falls when John was in grade school, and he tells me he was in second grade. He was born in Olympia, the family moved to Eugene when he was a toddler, then to Portland before relocating to Twin Falls. His oldest brother Duke was serving in the army, and Rosemary and Bill were in college when the family moved to Idaho. John was toward the end of the family and pretty much grew up in Twin Falls. His dad was a golf pro and had accepted a job at the beautiful Blue Lakes Country Club, appropriately located in the Snake River Canyon just a short distance from where years later, Evel Knievel would attempt his jump. So, even at a very young age, John had this Snake River Canyon connection.

After graduating from Twin Falls High in 1969, John attended College of Idaho in Caldwell on a partial football scholarship. An injury set him back, and he ended up graduating a semester later than originally intended.

"You graduated with a degree in journalism?" I ask, figuring he had his sights set on a career in sports journalism. I had started the interview with the misconception that he was the Sports Editor for the *Oregonian*, though John corrects me, telling me that he has been a sports editor, but that was not the main focus of his career.

"So, how did you get into the newspaper business?" I ask.

"I had no real plans until my senior year," John tells me. "I graduated with a degree in English Lit and a minor in Physical Education. I planned to teach high school English and coach."

When John graduated in December 1973, the job pool was flooded with prospective teachers, and he was getting a late start coming in halfway through the school year. He'd done his student teaching at Vallivue High School just outside of Caldwell and was told he would have to cut his hair if he wanted to teach. Things weren't moving toward a career in teaching.

During his senior year, John had done an internship at the *Idaho Free Press*. He'd always enjoyed writing, and teachers told him he was good at it. He had an uncle he admired who was a newspaper journalist. John was starting to think about a similar career. He took off for San Francisco where his uncle Bill Flynn worked at the *San Francisco Examiner*. After just a few months in San Francisco, John realized he didn't have the experience yet to get into the newspaper business in the Bay Area. He headed back to Caldwell.

He was working at the Grizzly Bear Pizza, trying to figure out his next move, when Jerry Snodgrass, Sports Editor for the *Idaho Free Press*, whom John knew from his earlier internship, came in and offered him a job as an assistant sports editor. When Jerry said he could pay him $140 a month, John told him he was already making $20 more than that at the pizza joint. Jerry matched the $160, and that's how John Killen became a newspaperman.

Just a couple of months into his new career, Jerry told John he was leaving to teach art. Much to his dismay, John was now Sports Editor at the *Idaho Free Press*. Shortly after this rapid ascent, feeling he wasn't quite ready for the position, John contacted his Twin Falls buddy, Paul Buker. John and Paul's friendship goes back to their grade school days, and John tells me that Paul was writing for the Twin Falls *Times-News*, doing a

Sunday sports section for the newspaper when he was just fifteen. Paul had recently graduated with a degree in journalism from the University of Oregon and was working part time in Eugene at the *Register-Guard*. John felt he was much more qualified for the sports editor position. He encouraged Paul to apply and told him he was perfectly willing to go back to the position he'd originally accepted. Paul came for an interview. "They hired him on the spot," John says.

This was July 1974, and Evel Knievel had already made a name for himself as a daredevil and showman. He was several years into promoting his Snake River Canyon jump, the Event of the Century, which would take place just two months after Paul and John joined their journalistic talents at the *Idaho Free Press*.

"Paul came up with the idea to cover the jump," John says. Evel was getting coverage from all over the world as he prepped for the jump, so it was only natural that a newspaper less than 150 miles northwest of Twin Falls would send a team of reporters to the jump site on the Snake River Canyon.

As part of the team, John and Paul were going home to Twin Falls, where they'd both grown up, to cover what might be the biggest event that little town had ever experienced. They had decided beforehand that Paul would be the primary reporter and John would concentrate on getting some photographs and writing a sidebar story. He describes himself as a mediocre photographer and his camera as completely lame.

"One of my memories was riding a press shuttle from the Holiday Inn to the launch site," John shares. "There were reporters and photographers on the shuttle from all over." He remembers hearing French spoken by some of his fellow passengers and other languages as well. "When we got to the launch site, the crowd was already pretty huge, and it just kept getting bigger as Paul and I tried to find a good vantage point."

"Did you notice any of the celebrities?" I ask. Evel had boasted that many would be there, including Elvis, Steve

McQueen, and Dustin Hoffman.

No Elvis, Steve, or Dustin, but John tells me the two celebrities he does remember seeing were Claudine Longet, the singer and actress who was married to Andy Williams (but separated), and Spider Sabich, the downhill skier. "I knew they had become a thing," John recalls, so he took note. A couple of years later, the couple made headlines when Claudine accidentally shot Sabich in some sort of spat.

I ask John if he remembers seeing Karl Wallenda, who was initially scheduled to do a tightrope walk across the canyon but had to scale it down to some kind of acrobatic act. John says he has no memory of that.

With their media credentials, he and Paul were in the area reserved for the press and had a good view of the Skycycle. John remembers being disappointed, even cynical, because he could see clearly that this was not a motorcycle.

He's not sure exactly how long they waited for Evel's arrival, but he does recall he arrived by helicopter with his wife and kids. After changing into his patriotic red, white, and blue leather jumpsuit in his on-site trailer, Evel came back to greet the crowd before he was hoisted up to the Skycycle and secured himself in the open cockpit. John and Paul were off to the east side of the launch pad, and John says they could only see Evel in profile. They weren't close enough to see his expression, and he'd strapped on his helmet for takeoff.

The thing that sticks in John's mind after the countdown is the sound. A blast of steam from the Skycycle that is, in fact, a steam-powered rocket. "Not a roar," John tells me, but a "loud blast of steam." The rocket shoots off the ramp, and John sees something coming out of the back. The rocket/Skycycle noses over. "Everyone realized that the jump had gone awry," John says. "People started screaming, and then the most terrifying thing happened—for us, anyway. Until then, the press corps and celebs had been separated from the main crowd by a chain-link fence. But when the crowd realized what had happened, they pushed the fence down and began to surge toward the canyon edge. For a few minutes (maybe just moments, but it seemed like minutes), we were pushed toward the edge of the canyon by the crowd, and I realized we could actually be pushed over the rim. At that point, I crouched and stood my ground, elbowing and pushing people aside as they rushed forward. The rest is kind of a blur." John recalls images of the Skycycle entangled in the branches of a tree along the canyon wall, thinks maybe he even got a few shots himself, but admits this might be a photograph he saw in the news after the event took place. He reminds me several times during the interview that he's attempting to bring up very old memories.

"Was it anger motivating the crowd?" I ask. I'd heard about and read news accounts about the destruction, the anger, the vandalism. John tells me at this point he didn't think it was anger that pushed the crowd toward the canyon's rim. They wanted to know what had happened. John says he thinks they were more scared and frightened.

"You were still there after Evel was rescued from down in the canyon and flown back up to the site? How was the crowd then?"

John sensed the crowd was more relieved than anything. So many who witnessed the blast off from the south canyon rim thought Evel was dead, and when he was brought back up to the launch site, he didn't appear to be seriously injured.

I ask John if he thinks Evel chickened out, an accusation made by many after the Snake River Canyon failure. John says he doesn't think that was the problem, and he was just glad when he saw Evel was okay. He and Paul continued to gather information and interview and eventually made their way back to the Holiday Inn.

When I ask if they rode back on the press bus, John says he can't remember exactly how they got back. They may have even walked. They rushed back to Nampa, wrote their stories, developed photos, and produced the coverage for the next edition.

116

"Do you still have copies of the article?" I ask eagerly.

I can hear John's chuckle over the phone. He tells me he did have boxes of clippings in the garage at a home where he lived in Lewiston. After two years at the *Idaho Free Press*, John went on to the *Lewiston Morning Tribune* for 11 years, then to Portland, working for the *Oregonian* for another 27 years. This is where John and his wife, Marlie, still live. One of their three sons works for the *Oregonian* as an award-winning photographer.

Our discussion now veers off from Evel. I'm very interested in John's 40+ years in the newspaper business that began with an internship in college and then continued with an offer while he was working at the Grizzly Bear Pizza. I'm always intrigued by a success story such as John's, when a person takes off on a path they never imagined. John tells me he did work as a sports writer in Lewiston, then as Bureau Chief at the *Oregonian*, then moving on to regional editor, then back to sports, and eventually to breaking news, supervising three editors and a dozen reporters. He tells me he worked with a great team of reporters. I can hear the admiration and respect in his voice. It's evident that John is in awe of these talented writers he supervised for many years. He pauses a moment and asks me if I know about imposter syndrome. Here's where I chuckle a bit, too. I've been posing as a writer for the past 17 years.

"So, what about those news clippings?" I circle back to our Evel discussion. "I'd love to read what you and Paul wrote and take a look at the *Idaho Free Press* coverage of the event."

John explains that when he and Marlie moved from Lewiston to Portland, they accidentally left several boxes of clippings in the garage at their old house. They went back to Lewiston a few years later and drove by the house, but had no luck in finding the clippings. The garage itself had been torn down.

John suggests several possible sources for newspaper archives as we finish our interview.

About a week later, John contacts me and says that he was able to find digital copies of the articles. He forwards them by email. No photos of Evel Knievel with John Killen credits, and in a text message John says, "I guess memory played tricks on me when I thought I remembered my photos being used." But the articles are well written, both his and Paul's. They each have a story with a by-line.

I am in awe of this kid in his early twenties who wanted to teach high school, who was just starting out as a journalist at the time of the Evel Knievel jump, this man who ended up with a four-decade-plus career in the newspaper business. No imposter involved here, John.

DAVID WHITEHEAD

David Whitehead wasn't born in Idaho, and his family always gives him a bad time about that, he tells me as we begin our phone interview. His family roots are planted deeply in the State. His great-grandfather on the Whitehead side of the family settled in Twin Falls in 1904, and his maternal grandmother's family, the Warbergs, arrived at about the same time. I tell David this is the same time my own maternal grandfather, Owen Buchanan, came to the Magic Valley to work for the Union Pacific Railroad. David's parents were both born in Idaho, his dad in Twin Falls and his mom in Rupert. His four siblings are all native Idahoans, too, but David, the oldest, was born at the Navy hospital in Memphis, Tennessee, while his dad served in the military. It was always his parents' intention to come back to Idaho, so when David was six months old and his dad was discharged from the Navy, they returned to their home state. David grew up in Twin Falls. He and his wife, Patti, now live in Whitefish, Montana, and he's visiting his daughter in Utah at the time of our call.

From a Facebook post, I knew that David had been at the Evel Knievel launch site while working with the phone company, Mountain Bell, or Ma Bell as it was affectionally known back then. This was long before cell phones, before the breakup of the big phone companies when one company prevailed and provided service for everyone in a particular area. Early predictions had over 200,000 showing up for Evel's

119

Snake River Canyon jump, necessitating some basic infrastructure be set up on the dry, windy south rim of the canyon where those who'd paid the fee to watch the jump would gather. I had read an article published in November 1974 in *Rolling Stone* magazine that claimed there were 200 chemical toilets,15 pay phones, and 30 drinking fountains set up. This, of course, was before people carried bottled water or Hydro Flasks, decorated with stickers and filled with ice water, everywhere they went.

When I throw these numbers out, David says he's sure there were more than 15 phones. The number that sticks in his mind is more like forty. He tells me a long plywood wall was built on site with pay phones mounted on both sides.

"How did you get started working for the phone company?" I ask. I know David graduated six years after I did from Twin Falls High School, so he would have been about twenty in the summer of 1974.

"I started working part-time, Saturdays and after school, while I was still in high school. I cleaned installers' work trucks and stocked them with phones and materials they'd need to install work orders. At that time, the phone company owned all the phones, so when people moved, I'd go pick up the phones."

I ask if someone in his family also worked for Ma Bell, and David tells me that both his dad and his uncle worked for the phone company. David left in 1977 to start his own company, a home and energy business. Whitehead Home and Energy is now owned and operated by David's youngest brother, Brent.

"Do you remember anything in particular during the days leading up to the Evel Knievel jump?" I ask.

He replies that people started noticing an influx of visitors, a rough-looking crowd, about one or two weeks before the jump, slowly at first but increasing as September 8 drew near. I ask if he ever saw Evel in town and tell David that Evel was known to frequent the Holiday Inn bar and the Blue Lakes Inn during the summer of '74. David doesn't drink, so he didn't hang out at either of these places. And no, he didn't see Evel until the day of the jump.

"Did you have any particular feelings about Evel Knievel before he started setting up for the big jump in Twin Falls?" David says he was aware of his reputation as a daredevil and knew he rode motorcycles but didn't see him as a great hero. He thought Evel was "interesting," though he wasn't a big fan.

I can't help but ask David about the Twin Falls schools and how these strange goings-on were handled by the school administrators because I know that his father-in-law, George Staudaher, was the superintendent of schools at the time. He was quoted in the *Rolling Stone* article from 1974 as saying, "School would absolutely begin on schedule, whether Evel Knievel jumps the canyon or not." David tells me that, yes, this sounds like his father-in-law. "He would never cancel school." The local Twin Falls *Times-News* reported that the high school had been running the water sprinklers constantly on the school lawn to discourage camping. David confirms this and tells me he doesn't know if they hired any additional security, but he was sure the administration was paying extra attention as these tough-looking visitors on motorcycles began appearing in town, searching for places to camp. Those grassy playgrounds at the grade schools might look tempting for pitching a tent or starting a bonfire.

Oddly, though I didn't know David before our phone interview, George Staudaher, who was the principal when I was in high school, provides another one of these hometown connections that seem to show up during each interview I do. I tell David a story about something that happened when I was in high school. One day, Mr. Staudaher called me into his office. I was only slightly concerned because I had been a student clerk in the office, and the principal knew I was a good student and that I wasn't known to cause any trouble. Mr. Staudaher was a tall, stern-faced, intimidating man, so I admit to a small amount of trepidation. I was surprised when he asked if I would be his daughter Patti's Confirmation sponsor. I told him I'd be honored. When I had asked David in an earlier communication if Patti could remember who her Confirmation sponsor was, he told me she didn't! But now, as we talk, I can feel his smile, even over the phone, when I tell him I remember Patti as a cute girl with dark hair and freckles. He tells me I'm right on with that description.

He shares that he and Patti met when they were 12, started dating at 15, and married right after high school. They celebrated their 50th anniversary on August 24, 2022. He still calls her his sweetheart.

So, this means that by the time Evel Knievel came to town, David, at the very young age of twenty, was two years into what has turned out to be a successful half-a-century union.

I ask him to tell me a little about being out at the jump site. "You must have spent a lot of time out there before the jump, installing the phones." David corrects me, telling me that he was part of the Mountain Bell crew assigned to the jump site, but he didn't install the phones; his assignment was to look after the Ma Bell microwave equipment that was being used by ABC television network. I knew from earlier research that there had been some serious controversy over the TV coverage because Evel insisted that it would only be shown on closed-circuit TV in movie theaters at the time of the jump and not on television network TV. Evel had evidently hired the ABC TV crews to do the filming, though all of this information was a little vague at the time of the jump. David tells me that there were three small trailers set up for the equipment, each about the size of a pickup bed, and this was where he and three other phone company employees spent their time when out at the jump site.

"You were out there early on the day of the jump?"

"Real early," he answers and describes how they had to be there early to get into the park because of the big crowds and traffic and to make sure all of the equipment was safe and operating.

"How did you feel about being out there? Was this something you had wanted to do?"

He didn't think at the time that it was that big of a deal, but he was young and curious and volunteered. At twenty, he was the youngest in the crew. He recalls that nobody really wanted the job.

I remind him that most of those out at the site had paid $25 to watch. "Didn't you feel like you and your co-workers were getting a freebee?"

David says he didn't until they were out at the site on the day of the jump. He describes the crowd as "the biggest I'd ever seen and not a scarier bunch." He'd never seen so many people in one place at one time. He was beginning to see this was a big deal. He recalls it took place on a weekend, and I confirm it was a Sunday afternoon. David tells me that "Once I got there, I was glad I was there and got paid to do it. Being a Sunday, I got paid extra. Patti and I had just purchased a house, and I was glad to have the overtime to help pay the bills."

That day, as David looked around at all the people, all the booths, he sensed this was something he needed to remember. He recalls climbing up on the equipment trailer to get a good view of the ever-increasing throng of spectators. He hadn't thought to bring a camera, and this was decades before a person could pull out a cell phone to record an event. Yet, he sensed it was something that would become part of Twin Falls history, and he wanted to remember what he saw.

David says he doesn't remember much about that time from early morning until the launch late that afternoon. "We sat around a lot." They spent most of the time just waiting and testing equipment. He does recall walking the line to check on the phones mounted on the plywood wall, but his memories of that day are mostly about the jump and the horrors of the aftermath.

"So, tell me about that. Do you have a memory of how Evel looked as he arrived and greeted the crowd just before the launch?"

David has a vivid memory of seeing Evel before he mounted

the Skycycle for takeoff. He describes his position with the Ma Bell crew at the ABC TV trailers as "right there at the bottom of the ramp."

He says Evel spoke to ABC staff and went up the ramp. "Solemn" is the word David uses to describe Evel. "Very solemn. He didn't look overly excited about doing it or afraid. He wasn't joking around." This was serious business.

The launch, as we all know now, was quick. The drogue chute, then the larger chute, came out, and the Skycycle took a dive straight down into the canyon.

"Did you think Evel was dead?" I throw out my standard question.

David says he didn't, because when the chute came out prematurely, the ascent was slowed, and he didn't feel Evel was in that much danger as he floated down. But he remembers clearly the surge of people in the crowd, the fence going down, spectators pushing to the canyon's rim. "It looked like the whole first line of people went over the edge." David and his crew were on the canyon side of the ABC equipment trailers, which were reasonably sturdy and protected them from being pushed forward by the out-of-control fans who had easily destroyed the chain-link fence along the rim. From this vantage point, David saw without obstruction, and he remembers the horror of the scene. People being pushed, so many dropping over the lip of the canyon.

At the time, David says he knew this would go down as the greatest loss of life at one time in the history of Twin Falls. It was only later that he would learn that there was another ledge just about 8 to 10 feet below. This ledge prevented those who had been forced over the south edge of the canyon from falling into the almost 500-foot abyss.

David remembers after Evel was brought back up out of the canyon, then quickly flown off site, he and his crew stayed with the equipment. Evel had his own security, but David and his crew, equipped with nothing more intimidating than tool belts, remained with their company's equipment.

"Did you feel cheated by Evel's failure to jump the canyon after the big buildup?" I ask, and David replies no, he didn't feel that at all. "But the people did." I assume he's talking about that rough-looking crowd, those who had paid the $25 to see Evel jump the canyon. "They started tearing things up. Burned pay phones and booths." He said the TV trailers weren't that close to where the phones had been set up, but they weren't concerned about the phones. The equipment on the trailers was far more valuable. So, they stood firm, guarding their equipment, witnesses to the ongoing fury, leaving only when things had settled down and were under control. "We never felt threatened," he tells me.

The destruction went on late into the night, but the next day, the Mountain Bell equipment used by ABC was still intact. David's crew did not return the following day, and he believes that Mountain Bell spread the overtime around among those who did the installations, those on hand the day of the jump, and those who were on site the following day. It soon became apparent, and word spread quickly that food booths, toilets, and pay phones had been destroyed, vandalized or set on fire.

I wondered about those old-fashioned coin-operated phones, though I guessed the plywood wall on which they'd been mounted had been torched. "Did the phone company make any money off those phones?" I ask.

"Destroyed," David tells me. I realize if there were any coins there, most likely they were picked up in the ash by some in the crown that had turned rowdy after Evel left them hanging. David tells me that if the phone company made any money, it would have been from collect calls made by people on site, charged on the receiving side by those accepting the calls. He doesn't know if this would have covered any damage, but he does remember long lines of people waiting to use the Mountain Bell phones the day of the jump.

David says it took a week or so to clean things up and

probably at least that long for all the visitors to leave town.

He repeats that the thing he remembers most vividly, an image that has stayed with him after all these years, is the people being pushed off the rim. When he learned that, amazingly, no one had died and only a few minor injuries were reported, he was relieved, though the memory of his initial fear remains intense.

The town returned to normal. Or perhaps not. David says the whole experience left a bad taste in many Twin Falls residents' mouths. No matter how you look at the ordeal, Evel left his mark on our little town. Evel Knievel and his jump over the Snake River Canyon, though unsuccessful, has become part of Twin Falls lore, etched into a collective memory.

An experience that Twin Falls will never forget. Part of our history, just as David predicted.

CHARLES COSGRIFF

The name **_Charles Cosgriff_** first came up in a conversation with John Killen. John told me that Charles became friends with Evel Knievel in Twin Falls and John thought maybe he would have some good stories he'd be willing to share. I found this prospect enticing and set out to find Charles. I didn't have to look far. I easily found him on Facebook and discovered, like me, he was now living in Boise. Though I was sure I'd never met Charles, I could see we shared over 50 Facebook friends, and I guessed if I sent a friend request, he would see the Twin Falls connection and accept my request, which he did.

I sent a private message, telling him about my earlier publication, my intention to republish for the 50th anniversary of Evel's Snake River Canyon jump, and that I planned on replacing the short stories in the book with first-hand accounts. I explained that John Killen had given me his name as a friend of Evel, saying he might have stories to share, and I would love to talk to him.

Charles agreed to meet and suggested we get together at O'Michael's Pub and Grill, a place on the road up to the Bogus Basin ski area where locals gather, often coming or going to the ski mountain, to grab a drink or snack, lunch or dinner. Neighbors also get together to meet friends and listen to live music on weekends.

I arrive several minutes early, wanting to make sure I'm not late. The front door leads into an enclosed entryway, where those down from the mountain head into the warmth and comfort of a place that's been around for over 50 years. The bar is off to the right, and the restaurant to the left. I take a few steps inside the bar, where all the activity seems to be taking place, and see, even though it is only 2:00 in the afternoon, the space is three-quarters full. Definitely a *Cheers* sort of vibe about it, people chatting at the bar and at several small tables scattered about the room. I've been here before to listen to local musicians; my brother-in-law Kenny Saunders has played here often. No live music this early in the day, but canned music is blasting a bit too loudly for my comfort. I glance around, looking for Charles just in case he has also arrived early. Based on his Facebook profile picture I'm confident I will recognize him. But it looks like I am the first to arrive. I cross back to the entry, then a few steps to the restaurant. It is completely deserted and though the music is drifting over from the bar, the room is not as dim and it is much more subdued. I hope Charles will agree this is a much better place for an interview.

While I wait, I think of a story I found in the Twin Falls *Times-News*, after I googled Charles Cosgriff. I came across a 1970 obituary of his grandmother Bessie, describing her as an early Twin Falls pioneer. The family originally arrived in Twin Falls in the early 1900s. The article says that Charles's grandparents were married in Butte, Montana, and I had wondered if this was some kind of connection because Evel Knievel grew up in Butte. I also recall a *Sports Illustrated* article, published in 1974, that I clipped while I was doing my earlier research for the original Evel Knievel book. I've tucked the article into my bag. There is a sidebar in the article, telling about a golf game between Evel Knievel and Chuck Cosgriff, who is described as the town's best golfer. Also joining in the golf game were Evel's sons Robbie, 12, and Kelly,13. Evel's daughter, Tracey, 9, and his wife Linda, 31, were also along to "run messages, fetch lost balls and clubs and zoom back to the clubhouse at the master's whim for more gin and tonics." Not sure that this would fly in the 2020s, but this is a quote from the 1974 article.

Charles arrives shortly and immediately agrees the bar is too crowded, dark, and loud. I offer to get him a drink, thinking I'll be clever and suggest a gin and tonic. But, before we even settle down at a table in the restaurant, which doesn't appear to have any service at this hour, he tells me that he and Evel quit drinking at about the same time. So, we both order a soft drink from the bar, and I feel a bit relieved at this.

When my diet coke and his soda water are delivered from the bar to the restaurant side, I pull out my iPad, ready to ask if I can record our conversation. I've also brought my spiral notebook and pen if Charles is uncomfortable with recording our conversation.

One of the first things he tells me is that he is still friends with members of Evel's family and doesn't want to be associated with anything that might hurt the family. I haven't even brought up the idea of recording our conversation yet, and I set my iPad, pen and paper aside. So, I don't have Charles's exact words, but he lets me know that he's aware there are still bad feelings among some locals about Evel Knievel's time in Twin Falls. And he doesn't want to be part of a hit job on his friend, who passed away in 2007 at the age of 69.

I have to pause for a moment and rethink what I'm hoping to gain from this conversation. My original story about Evel Knievel was fiction, told from the point of view of a ten-year-old boy, and Evel never actually appears in the story. He is not portrayed as the hero, but now, as we sit at O'Michael's, I'm running through the highlights of the story in my head, questioning if Charles or the Knievel family would find anything in the story offensive.

I describe the general content and feel of the fictitious story and explain I will be removing the short stories for the second edition and replacing them with first-hand accounts, and that's why I'm hoping he will consider talking to me about his friendship with Evel. I also explain that the first-hand accounts I'm working on, based on interviews I've already done, are focusing more on real Twin Falls people and how the arrival of Evel impacted their lives, or at the least added a bit of excitement to the summer of '74. But, still, I'm initially a bit uncomfortable with continuing our conversation. Yet, as Charles and I talk, it seems we have plenty to share, the first being our families with such strong Idaho roots. I tell him about finding his grandmother's obit in the local newspaper, point out his grandparents were married in Butte, and then ask if there is an Evel Knievel connection. He seems curious but tells me that he wasn't aware of any connection or even the fact that his grandparents were married in Butte.

Charles tells me that Evel was above all a showman, a performer, but there was much more to the man than that. He had a soft spot for kids and often visited sick children in the hospital. Evel had spent substantial time in hospitals due to his many injuries and he always made time to visit the children in the hospitals in the various places he performed. Even though he performed dangerous live-threatening stunts for entertainment, he promoted safety helmets. He was an advocate for mandatory motorcycle helmets and extended his support for helmets to kids on bikes.

Though Charles has expressed his concerns about my project, he shares a story about a call he received from Evel who was phoning from jail. "Well, I really messed up this time," he told Charles. I don't push on this; I just let Charles talk. Since I haven't requested that we record our conversation, I don't have his exact words, but I sense by telling me about this phone call, he's willing to admit that Evel was no saint.

I'm aware of a 1977 book written by Sheldon Saltman, Evel's promoter for the jump in Twin Falls. It was scathing, portraying Evel in an unflattering way. After the book came out, Evel took a thug along with him to talk to Shelly, and let's just say that

Shelly emerged from that encounter in not the greatest shape. He pressed charges. Evel eventually agreed he'd been less than gracious and spent some time in jail. I'm guessing it was during this time that Charles got the call. The book, *Evel Knievel on Tour*, by Sheldon Saltman, is available at the Boise Public Library, but it is listed as non-circulating, which means it can't be checked out of the library. I know the publisher eventually pulled the book after the threat of a lawsuit from Evel's attorneys, so copies are rare. There are other published books that paint Evel Knievel as a true American hero. Perhaps the truth is somewhere in between these two portrayals.

I know, from my earlier reading, that the Saltman incident resulted in several of Evel's promotional contracts being canceled.

Charles and I move on to more neutral territory. We share our family backgrounds and common acquaintances. As I guessed, Charles knew John Killen through John's dad who was the golf pro at the Blue Lakes Country Club. When I ask if it's true what *Sports Illustrated* said about him being the town's best golfer, Charles tells me he still holds a Blue Lakes course record after all these years.

We talk a bit about living in Boise. I came to Boise in the early seventies, and Charles a few years later. The family sold the Cosgriff sign business many years ago, but he still likes to remain active and has been selling luxury cars at a local Boise dealer, just part-time now. He speaks with admiration and affection of his wife Judie, who I know from my Facebook sleuthing is a talented artist. I also learn during our conversation, that they lived in the big Lion House on Harrison Boulevard, but have downsized from there. For those not familiar with Boise and the Halloween tradition on Harrison Boulevard, if you are ever in Boise for the Holiday, this is where the action takes place. Charles and his wife were part of this neighborhood celebration, and the Lions standing sentinel on the massive porch are always decorated for the holidays, a tradition established by the Cosgriffs.

I'm still cautious about throwing out my standard questions about Evel, inquiring about the day of the Snake River Canyon jump, or delving into Charles's personal feelings about any of that. If we do get into this territory, I want to record or at least take notes. And I know that when exploring the nebulous world of memory, fact and personal recollections often collide. So, I want to get it right.

We end our conversation with me giving him a copy of my original *Evel Knievel Jumps the Snake River Canyon.* I tell him if he reads the story and feels comfortable with the way I have portrayed Evel in my fictitious story, I hope he will be willing to talk to me again.

I'm not sure he will be in touch, but I don't leave our meeting with a bad feeling about our conversation. A couple of weeks later, Charles sends me a message, saying he enjoyed the book and would like to meet again. We agree to get together at O'Michael's the following week and talk.

This time I ask if I can record and he agrees. I ask if he prefers to be called Charles, Chuck—as he was in the *Sports Illustrated* article—or Charlie, and he says he prefers Charles. I tell him again my other interviews have been as much about family as about Evel Knievel, the emphasis always coming down to what it was like to be a citizen of Twin Falls during the challenging '70s when Evel Knievel came to town. We talk a bit more about family and Charles tells me his paternal family is from Kentucky. His grandfather's brother had a distillery and Charles's grandfather ordered a barrel of whiskey to be delivered to Twin Falls. Unfortunately, a 50-gallon barrel ended up in the Snake River, due to a brake failure on the ferry. I remember stories from my own grandparents about the early days of the community before there was a bridge spanning the canyon. People and supplies were ferried across the river, after a steep ascent down into the canyon. Evidently, not everything loaded onto the ferry arrived safely on the other side of the canyon.

Charles moves on to share details of his childhood. He says his parents traveled often when he was young—he was an only child and he spent substantial time with his grandmother, who lived on 7th Avenue in the old part of Twin Falls. My maternal grandparents lived on 8th Avenue, and my paternal grandparents had a home later in their lives on 6th Avenue. I grew up on 9th Avenue. We share memories of Thursday night band concerts in City Park off 6th Avenue. We are literally finding common ground. I recall, as we talk about how grandparents were an important part of our growing up, that Bobby Knievel was raised by his grandparents.

Charles tells me his grandfather, C. P. Cosgriff, who passed away before Charels was born, founded Cosgriff Outdoor Advertising Company in the early 1900s, and the business was eventually handed down to Charels's dad, Melbrine. Charles took over due to the early passing of his father when he was 18 and studying at the University of Nevada. By then, the business had expanded beyond just outdoor advertising and had added several locations, including offices in Nevada, so Charles was able to remain in Nevada and continue his studies.

After a while, I ask Charles to tell me about his first encounter with Evel Knievel.

Charles said he was in the Twin Falls office, probably in the early 70s, and Evel himself came in to order some signs, not billboards, but smaller signs to put on the Skycycle and the launch pad. Charles recalls him announcing, "I'm Evel Knievel, and I'm going to jump the Snake River Canyon."

"So, you knew who he was? You were aware of the impossible stunt he was planning? What did you think?"

Charles says he knew about him from what he was reading in the papers, and like many in town, he was making jokes with his friends. But, Charles remembers, even during that initial conversation, "I enjoyed talking to him and we got to laughing right off the bat." Evel told Charles about his plans for the motocross races and said he was going to build "a track with the most mud and the biggest dips of any motocross that's ever been." Evel told him this would be the toughest track ever built. As Charles retells the story of their first meeting he chuckles at the memory.

During that first encounter, according to Charles, Evel asked if there were any good golf courses in the area.

Oh, this was right up your alley, I'm thinking. After my first meeting with Charles, I had found numerous articles in the Twin Falls *Times-News,* listing results of local golf tournaments back in the 70s and 80s, and I know that the *Sports Illustrated* article touting Chuck Cosgriff as the town's best golfer isn't an exaggeration. Charles was known for his skills on the golf course, had made a name for himself, and he had played on the golf team for the University of Nevada.

So, he suggested the Blue Lakes Country Club down in the Snake River Canyon, told Evel it was really nice, and asked if he wanted to go down there. Evel said, "I'd love to," and they set up a golf date, the first of many. Later, about a week before the Twin Falls jump, Evel invited Charles to a celebrity golf tournament in Butte and flew him up in his Lear jet. Here he met celebrity athletes of the day, including Joe Louis and Bobby Riggs. During this trip for the pre-jump golf tournament, he mingled with others at a get-together at Evel's home in Butte. He says there were so many people there, that he didn't get much time to talk to Evel, but he did have a conversation with engineer Bob Truax, a 24-year Veteran of the United States Navy, who had been enlisted to design the steam-powered engine that would propel the Skycycle across the Snake River Canyon. Even then, as the jump approached, Charles says that Truax was encouraging Evel to cancel the jump, that Truax didn't believe the Skycycle was ready. Truax shared his concerns about the chute. He told Charles that he saw problems with it opening too soon or too late. If too late, according to Bob Truax, the skycycle might end up across the canyon in Jerome.

"Was Evel a good golfer?" I ask.

Charles laughs and tells me, "To begin with, he was terrible."

When they played those early games in Twin Falls, there was plenty of room for improvement, according to Charles.

"You always won?" I don't imagine that would set well with Evel, a man who always saw himself as a winner.

"I gave him strokes," Charles tells me, then asks if I play golf or if I'm familiar with how it is scored. I admit my knowledge of the game is limited, and Charles explains how he would add extra strokes to his own score to even things up and give Evel a better chance. He gave Evel throws, which means the less skillful golfer could pick up the more advanced player's ball once during the game and throw it. Again, Charles laughs and tells me that one time while playing on the course in Twin Falls, "I get on the green, he walks up and throws my ball in the Snake River." I get the impression they had some fun times together.

After the jump, after Charles moved to Boise, Evel came up to visit him several times, and they'd share a round of golf at the Crane Creek Country Club.

By then, Charles explains, Evel was a much better golfer. "He took some lessons from some pretty good pros." By the time they were playing in Boise at Crane Creek, in the late 70s and 80s, he'd really improved. It seems no matter what challenges the man took on, he always attempted to improve his skills.

"He was competitive, then?" I ask.

"Yes, very much."

"Some betting on the games?" I inquire. I figure a man whose entire life is a gamble would be tossing out a bet or two on a competitive game like golf.

There were bets, not always serious, sometimes in the millions. Charles says he still has a check that Evel wrote after one of their Blue Lakes games in Twin Falls. "It was dated the day after the jump, and Evel told me after that if he didn't make it, he didn't care what I did with the check." With a shake of his head and a grin he repeats, "I still have the check."

"How much was the check for?"

Charles ponders the question and tells me he is not sure since he never cashed it. As he recalls, it wasn't that much, but truly a valuable, but more importantly, a very personal piece of memorabilia.

"What did you call him?" I ask, thinking maybe Evel was just his stage name. I knew he'd grown up in Butte as Bobby Knievel.

"I called him Evel." Charles goes on to tell me the story of how Evel Knievel got his name. He was in the local jail in Butte, after some minor infraction, with a well-known and frequent visitor, William Knofel, who had been dubbed Awful Knofel. It seemed appropriate that Mr. Knievel should be known as Evel Knievel, and it stuck. Later, after he began performing as a motorcycle daredevil and stuntman, Evel adopted the name legally, spelling it with an "e," so it wouldn't sound quite so evil.

"Do you think this is a true story or just a myth?"

"Probably true," Charles replies.

"What did his wife call him?"

She called him Evel, too, as far as Charles can remember, yet he hesitates on his answer and admits he didn't know Linda that well, that he got to know Evel's second wife, Krystal, better. Linda spent little time in Twin Falls, staying back home in Butte to take care of their children. "I remember she was quiet and religious." He describes her as a nice person, but not interested in being in the limelight.

Charles tells me when he visited the family in Butte, he recalls that Evel had jumps set up in the backyard for the kids. He remembers that Robbie was especially skilled. He went on to become a professional stuntman and performer like his dad. (Sadly, just a couple of months after Charles and I talked, Robbie Knievel passed away from pancreatic cancer.)

Charles goes on to share additional stories of adventures with Evel. He shows me a picture of a bright yellow Cadillac station wagon, pulled up on his phone. "He ordered this Cadillac, the only one ever built, and Evel told me, 'I'm gonna show it to you, I'm gonna bring it down.' So, he shows up with this station wagon." Then, Evel invited Charles to go down to Jackpot,

Nevada, to play a game of golf with some Twin Falls locals and casino investors before the new course at Cactus Pete's was opened to the public. They were speeding down the road at 100 mph—"everywhere he went, he drove 100 mph"—in this bright yellow Cadillac station wagon, when a tire blew out! The station wagon was loaded down with golf equipment, but, unfortunately, not a spare tire in sight. Being that it was a one-of-a-kind automobile, they figured it would be impossible to find a replacement tire. Eventually, they got a ride to Jackpot with other Twin Falls friends. Charles doesn't go into detail about the golf game itself or how they resolved the problem with the yellow Cadillac station wagon. But, with Evel, it seems the ride to get there was as much an adventure as the planned event.

Charles references the true incident of the baloney display at Swensen's Market that I included in my book. The display implied that Evel Knievel was full of baloney and offered him a twenty-pound baloney if he successfully jumped the canyon. Charles says that Evel told him, "I went into Swensen's, grabbed the biggest piece of baloney I could find and chased Mr. Swensen around the store." Charles says he's not sure if this actually happened, but we are both laughing now at the image.

"He told stories, didn't he," I say.

"Oh, yeah."

"Could you tell the difference, between when he was lying or just telling stories?"

"Not really. Not really." We are both laughing again.

Charles has other stories about hanging out with Evel and his celebrity friends both before and after the jump. He drops some names like Porter Wagoner, Roy Acuff, and Peter Marshall, famous back in the 70s and 80s. He tells me about spontaneous trips to places like Nashville, Tennessee. The invitation to Nashville didn't allow Charles much prep time. Evel called about 7:00 p.m., asking if he could be ready to leave at 11:00.

The flight in Evel's private King Air, allowed for a couple of stops on the way to Nashville, one in Kansas City to visit Robert

Docking, a candidate for governor whom Evel was endorsing. Charles recalls the dinner where Evel picked up the tab, and Charles offered to pay the tip. He put out what he thought was a generous and reasonable amount. Evel pushed it back and slapped down a couple of hundred-dollar bills, commenting that when you travel with Evel, this is how you tip. Charles joked that he'd pay for the meals from here on out, and Evel could leave the tip.

He recalls getting together with some of Evel's friends and business associates brought into Twin Falls for the publicity and promotions that were needed for the Idaho event. A special memory is sitting next to Bob Arum at the Turf Club, suggesting that the big-time sports promoter try the lamb chops as they were especially great. Arum was a celebrity in his own right, the head of Top Rank Inc., a boxing promo company that did events for well-known sports figures, including Muhammed Ali. Making small talk with Arum is something Charles will never forget.

I pull the conversation back to Evel's time in Twin Falls just before the jump and ask Charles if they ever talked about what might happen, or if Evel ever spoke of his fear of failure in his attempt to jump the Canyon.

Charles says they may have laughed about it a little, but no, they didn't really talk about it. He didn't want "to stir things up." I wonder if this was one of the reasons they became friends; Charles didn't ask him about his professional life. This seemed to be off the table when they got together. I get the impression that they were friends because Charles didn't ask about the jump, that they had fun and enjoyed time together that had nothing to do with the Twin Falls Snake River Canyon jump.

"Did you notice a change in his demeanor as the time for the jump approached?"

At first, Charles says no, but then gives it more thought and says he did notice Evel get "a little impatient with the press." He tells me that as the time got closer to the scheduled jump, he did seem a "little nervous, but he never expressed fear."

"Do you think he thought he was going to die?" I prod gently, to which Charles replies, 'Have you seen videos of his Caesars Palace jump?" This took place several years before Charles' first meeting Evel in Twin Falls. Evel broke just about every bone in his body according to the possibly exaggerated press reports, and he spent around a month in the hospital, with some accounts saying he was in a coma. Many thought this would be his last jump.

I nod vaguely as I visualize the Caesars Palace jump. Both Charles and I are aware that the man lived with the constant threat of death. Each stunt he attempted could possibly be his last.

When I ask about the day of the Twin Falls jump, Chares tells me he was there, but as part of the crowd. The area up close was reserved for the press and Evel's team of publicists, promoters, handlers, and engineers. But Charles had no better seat than anyone else in the crowd, so his view wasn't that great, especially with the enormous crowd that had gathered along the rim, many jostling for a more advantageous position to witness this historic event. He guessed those who saw it on the live theater feed, and later on TV, probably had a better view.

I ask what he remembers about the event and what happened on site after the jump.

Like most witnesses, Charles's memory of the jump is that it all happened quickly. Then after, "Chaos and Panic," is how he describes the scene. "Nobody knew what was going on."

When I ask if he thought Evel chickened out and deployed the chute himself, he replies, "No." If he had wanted to, he could have canceled the jump, Charles explains. Even the designers of the skycycle were concerned there would be problems as there had been with two earlier test runs. Evel could have thrown that out as an excuse for canceling the jump. But, he never did. He said he would do it, and he was true to his word, something always important to Evel. After the failed jump, Bob Truax, the chief engineer for the Skycycle's steam-powered engine, took the blame. A malfunction, not Evel's fault.

Charles can't recall if he saw Evel again before he left Twin Falls to head back home to Butte, but they would get together many times after that, often in Boise.

As our interview winds down, I sense that Charles wants to leave me with some understanding of Evel as a friend, as a person who was much deeper than what the press portrayed, though it was often Evel as a self-promotor who eagerly fed the media.

Again, he shares with me Evel's passion as an advocate for motorcycle helmet safety, and his testifying to support mandatory helmet laws. Although when Charles tells me about Evel's advocacy, he also tells me he was paid, as expert witnesses often are. Earlier in our conversation, Charles had admitted, with a touch of humor, that Evel was always "gonna make a dollar after everything he did."

He tells me that Evel was a good, down-to-earth man, always available for kids, and always willing to sign autographs for fans. "He could be a jerk, trying to cause controversy." But, that was all part of being an entertainer, a performer, a persona he developed with great skill.

Charles shows me some images on his phone, paintings that Evel was said to have done in his later years, and then a photo of a gold pendant belonging to Charles's wife Judie, gifted to her from Evel. One morning, as the friends were having coffee, Judie noticed the pendant Evel was wearing, remarked how much she loved it, and he took it off from around his neck and handed it to her.

Later I will try to find information on Evel as an artist, but have little luck in verifying if these paintings are authentic. But I understand the point Charles is making is that there was more to the man than the showman, the entertainer, the one who had to be the center of attention when he performed his daredevil stunts for a large, often adoring crowd.

As we end our conversation, I want to ask Charles what he wishes people would remember about Evel, but before I can even get the question out, he says, "He was a good guy, a whole lot more good characteristics than bad."

And this is the way he remembers his friend, as he reflects on their times together. "I never cross that canyon that I don't think of him," he adds thoughtfully.

RITA DELANEY

Evel Knievel might have been described as a man's man because of his daring motorcycle stunts, and his death-defying performances certainly appealed to young boys who saw him as a superhero. It wasn't surprising then, that those who had agreed to be interviewed about their Twin Falls experience during the summer of Evel Knievel were all men who had been 20-somethings in 1974.

I'd also heard and read that Evel was a ladies' man, a charismatic celebrity who attracted young women no matter where he went. I was curious what a woman who'd met him during the time he spent in Twin Falls might have to say about Evel Knievel.

Charles Cosgriff suggested I contact **Rita Delaney**, who had already been on my radar because of a Facebook post following the death of Evel's son, Robbie Knievel. Rita extended her sympathy to the family and reflected on what a cute little boy Robbie had been when she met him in Twin Falls.

I contacted Rita and she agreed to meet for coffee. Rita, like many who'd grown up in the Magic Valley, had migrated to the Boise area and was now living in Meridian. We decided to get together at a coffee shop in Eagle.

Rita, an attractive woman with blonde hair and a friendly smile, looks much younger than her age, which I will not reveal. Based on her being in her early to mid-twenties at the time Evel first started showing up in town, I know she is about my age. She tells me, though she didn't grow up in Twin Falls, she had Twin Falls friends, lived there for many years as an adult, and enjoyed the active life with her husband Mike and four of her children who were born there. She grew up on a farm south of Filer, a small agricultural community west of Twin Falls, and graduated from Filer High School. Her family originally came from Arkansas; her dad arrived in Idaho in the late 1930s to look for work, which he found at the Reichert family farm. Eventually, he sent for his wife and three toddlers, who, Rita reflects with a smile, traveled to their new home in the back of a pickup truck. Clyde later acquired his own farm south of Filer on the Salmon Tract where they grew potatoes, beans, wheat, hay, and corn. Clyde and his wife, Lena, added three more children to the family in Idaho. Rita's father passed away suddenly when she was just 12. Her mom became a young widow with six children, two still at home. Rita speaks with admiration of how her mom went to work, how she raised her kids alone, and how, despite the hardships, led a fulfilling life, traveling the United States, as far as Hawaii, and eventually to Europe. She also enjoyed all that the Twin Falls area had to offer. Lena was a big fan of the College of Southern Idaho Golden Eagles basketball team. One year, along with her best friend, Darlene Frazier, she was honored as Booster of the Year.

When I ask Rita how she met Evel, she tells me it was through her husband, the late Mike Gray, who served as Knievel's liaison, a go-between with the community, helping Evel secure a location for his launch, assisting him in maneuvering through the maze of necessary permits with the BLM, county, and city, and managing local arrangements that would be required for the jump to take place. As we talk, I recall that Mike's mother, Catherine, was a friend of my mom's. Catherine owned a business working with children who needed additional tutoring and diagnosis to address reading difficulties. I know she helped my youngest brother Brian who is a talented artist and dyslexic, a not-so-commonly known condition back then.

Rita tells me she first met Mike through her best friend, Joyce Tegan, who'd become acquainted with Mike when he was working in Washington D.C. as an Administrative Assistant for Idaho Congressman Ralph Harding. When Joyce visited Washington, Mike showed her the sights of the city.

Joyce introduced Mike and Rita and they ran into each other from time to time after that because of mutual friends. Several years later their paths crossed again when they were both single parents working in Twin Falls. Rita was in the ads department at the *Times-News*, and Mike was managing the Twin Falls Title and Trust. Mike came into the newspaper office one day, and, according to Rita, "they finally broke the ice and engaged in conversation." After that encounter, he called and invited Rita to go to the County Fair. Three weeks later, they married. Between them, they had three young children, Tina, 3, Mitch, 2, Tim,1, and 9 months later they added another, Travis.

She goes on to tell me the story that Mike often told about the day he met Evel in Twin Falls.

Mike had graduated from St. John's University in Minnesota and started law school at the University of Idaho. One day, his dad, Gordon, called and asked Mike if he would come back home to become President of a family business. Mike returned to Twin Falls and joined the Twin Falls Title and Trust Company, founded by his dad. One day, Mike stepped out of the office on Shoshone Street and noticed a man lying in the back of a station wagon parked on the street. The window was cracked to allow some fresh air to circulate, and there was no one else in the car. Mike approached.

"Hi, I'm Mike Gray," he introduced himself. "How can I help you?"

The man stirred, looked up at Mike, and said, "I'm Evel Knievel, and I'm looking for a canyon to jump."

"Well," Mike said, "I just might have a canyon for you."

A friendship developed from there, and Mike and Evel began working together to secure a location for the jump as Mike guided Evel in navigating through the various channels for permits that would be required. Mike was involved in local politics, a member of the City Council and Fair Board, and had numerous connections in town and a reputation that would be beneficial for Evel to establish credibility. One of the things that stands out in Rita's memory is the calls that Evel made to Mike during the several years leading up to the jump in 1974. One of the reasons these memories are especially vivid is that they always came at about 3:00 in the morning. Back then, it was the norm for a landline phone to sit on the nightstand in the bedroom, so Rita was always awakened by these calls. She explains that Evel had so many injuries from his stunts and had difficulties sleeping, so it seemed natural for him to pick up the phone at any time, night or day, with apparently no considera-tion for the recipient of the call, or any concerns that he might awaken a sleeping wife. Rita laughs and tells me one of the things she especially remembers as Mike talked to Evel, was that he kept slapping her leg, not for any particular reason other than it was just a reflex reaction or perhaps a case of the nerves while conversing with Evel.

Of course, Rita could only hear one side of the conversation: Mike repeating over and over, 'Okay, buddy, okay."

"Why do you think Mike kept taking these middle-of-the-night calls?" I ask her.

"It was Evel," she answers with a shrug and a laugh and perhaps the memory of something exciting and extraordinary that had invaded the sleepy little community and the lives of so many families in town.

"When did you first meet Evel in person?" I ask.

"Mike invited him over for breakfast one morning at the house. I knew he liked bacon, crisp."

'Okay! Crisp bacon," I exclaim. Have I finally found my own

common ground with Evel?

Rita says she was surprised that the first thing he asked for when he came in was a couple of shots of whiskey. She said this was the way he started each day.

I'm picturing the table set with fine china, juice glasses, napkins, and a full set of flatware. I doubt there was a shot glass perched on the table. From the few minutes I've spent with Rita, I get the impression she'd set a nice table. She confirms that she did indeed set a nice table for Evel. She just shakes her head and laughs again. "No, he didn't notice any of that."

"What was your first impression?" I ask.

"He was intimidating." He came in bigger than life, wielding his signature gold-tipped cane, encrusted with diamonds, as much a prop as it was a necessary physical support due to his many injuries. "Really good looking. He had a sexy way about him." She admits she was a bit afraid of him. Here he comes in flashing his fancy cane, demanding a couple of shots of whiskey. The man knew how to make an entrance. And, yes, he was charismatic, friendly, and engaging.

Rita tells me a story that especially stands out in her Evel Knievel memories, something that happened shortly after they met him.

"Mike and I were planning a trip to visit his brother in California. Of course, we were eager to stop in Las Vegas to see the lights and excitement that the city brought in the early '70s. When Mike mentioned to Evel that we would be gone for a week and told him where we were going, he immediately told Mike to go to one of the newest and most luxurious casinos"—Rita can't remember exactly which casino, but believes it was the MGM Grand— "and ask for Howie." Evel told them he would let Howie know they were coming.

"Like two country bumpkins, after arriving at the hotel, Mike stepped up to the front desk and announced, 'Evel Knievel sent us for Howie.' Quickly, a dark complexion handsome man, looking like he was straight from GQ magazine, appeared. He asked us about our time frame and what shows we would enjoy. Shortly after checking in, we were sent our agenda for the two days in Vegas. It included our complimentary room, all meals, 2 shows per night with VIP seating at various venues." Rita remembers seeing Johnny Carson, Engelbert Humperdinck, Suzanne Somers, and Kenny Rogers.

"It was a dream weekend living like the rich and famous," Rita says.

She goes on to tell me about Evel's regular visits with the family in Twin Falls. Her boys especially loved him. Every time he came over, he brought a bag of Evel Knievel toys for the boys and the neighborhood kids. Of course, that was a big hit with all the little boys in the neighborhood and made Rita and Mike's boys feel quite important. She also tells me that after the first unmanned test Skycycle was shot off over the canyon, the severely damaged vehicle was hauled back into town and stored in their garage. Her oldest son, Tim, an entrepreneur at a very young age, lined all the neighborhood kids up and charged them 25 cents each to get a peek at Evel's Skycycle!

On occasion, when Evel was in town, he'd invite his friends to join him for a ride in his jet. He had a loyal pilot named Watcha McCollum, who would sweep down into the canyon, often leaving his passengers' stomachs somewhere behind. "I've never been so scared in my life," Rita says. It was a frightening experience, but so in character for Evel to want to share his love of adventure and danger with his friends. Memories that are still with Rita over 50 years later.

Rita remembers that Evel liked to gather friends at the Alley, a bar in the south part of town. He'd spontaneously call and invite friends to join him.

"Did the wives get invited too?" I ask.

At times, Rita went along with Mike, but she doesn't recall many other wives, and she doesn't think Evel was especially respectful of women. I know he had a reputation as a ladies' man, and there was talk around town.

I get up the nerve and ask Rita if he ever made a pass at her.

"More on that later," she answers with a tilt of her head, her voice indicating there is more to come in her personal story.

Rita recalls her friendship with Evel's wife, Linda, though by most accounts she spent little time in Twin Falls. "She was absolutely beautiful," Rita says, "with porcelain skin and dark hair. So, so sweet." According to Rita, when she was around, Evel pretty much told her what to do and was upset when things didn't go as he planned. She remembers a time when they were all out at the motocross track, Evel barking out one demand after another to his wife. As the time for the jump approached, Evel got especially impatient, not just with Linda, but with anyone involved in the event. He wanted everything to be perfect and in place for the jump, and if that wasn't your goal, then you were out of there.

The night before the jump, Evel threw a big party at the Canyon Springs Inn. Rita recalls seeing celebrities including Steve McQueen, Ali MacGraw, Claudine Longet, Spider Sabich, Don King, Bob Arum, Margaux Hemingway, and a number of minor celebrities who were in town for the jump. She can't remember if Linda was at the party. It was more likely she was with the children in the hotel room.

Later that night, back home, Rita recalls gazing out through the back sliding door of their home toward the jump site. It appeared the whole countryside along the canyon was burning. The event had brought some unruly spectators to town. Mike took off to check it out. He didn't sleep that night. As it turned out, a large, rowdy group, several hundred of the thousands camped on site had gone on a rampage because of a shortage of beer, vandalizing trucks and vendor booths, looting beer, and torching concession stands. The numerous bonfires blazing along the rim may have also contributed to this hellish scene. The destruction went on, according to news articles, until dawn when it was somewhat under control. Security was able to keep the mob from destroying the launch pad and Skycycle.

On the day of the much-anticipated event, Mike and Rita flew from the Holiday Inn to the jump site in a helicopter provided by Evel. The late Margaux Hemingway, granddaughter of Ernest Hemingway, accompanied them. As they waited on site, Rita stayed with Linda and the kids in the motorhome, away from the commotion of the crowd until it was time for Evel to be hoisted up to the Skycycle and prepare for the launch.

Many of those on the security team hired by Evel seemed to have disappeared, perhaps feeling the job was too risky. Shortly before the jump, knowing he had to have security on duty, Evel took a bold move and rode his motorcycle into the middle of the Hell's Angels campsite. They had been blamed—most likely unjustly—for the destruction of the previous night and early morning. After telling them he needed their help, they stepped up in an attempt to protect Evel, control the crowds, and prevent eager spectators from getting too close to the canyon rim. Rita still remembers the image of those tough-looking men in their leathers and chains, forming a line with their hands locked around each other's wrists, protecting the rim and the danger that threatened those who might think getting closer was a good idea.

Rita describes others in the crowd, particularly two girls who she had seen accompany Evel at various times and who likely believed they held a special place in his heart. One of them, a beautiful blonde, was crying and, at one point, even down on her knees praying as she gripped the wire fence along the canyon wall. Rita remembers an awkwardness, feeling uncomfortable, particularly with the spectacle of these women as she waited with Evel's wife and children for what many believed would be the daredevil's last stunt.

"Can you describe what you observed," I ask, "the emotions of the family as Evel settled into the cockpit of the Skycycle ready to shoot across the canyon?"

Kelly, the oldest, wanted to watch, but Robbie couldn't. Rita remembers the dark-haired, handsome little boy curled up in a ball on the ground with his hands over his eyes, fearful for his dad. "He was so scared." Rita doesn't specifically recall Tracey's reaction, but imagines "she was hanging on and hiding behind her mother." Linda seemed, to Rita, conditioned to show little emotion, but after the Skycycle launched and then quickly took a dive, she was near panic. Rita remembers giving her a big hug.

"Did everyone think he was dead?" I ask.

Word came back quickly that he was okay, that he was being retrieved by a crew waiting in the river in a boat, part of a rescue plan in case Evel ended up in the Snake River. Later they would learn he'd landed in the lava rocks on the same side of the canyon from which he'd launched.

"Do you think Evel chickened out?"

"No," Rita answers without hesitation. "They had worked too hard to make this happen." She remembers when Evel was brought back up by helicopter, and he was sitting in the motor home on a bar stool, face bloody and scratched—she doesn't recall if this was before or after he greeted the crowd and the press—he told relieved family and friends, "You don't know how bad I wanted to see the other side of that canyon." She knew he hadn't aborted the jump.

Some of those in the crowd believed otherwise, and the destruction and vandalism that had begun the previous night continued, leaving the site looking like what many described as a war zone by the end of the day. The remaining concession stands were knocked down and torched. Equipment set up to provide communication and sanitation services was destroyed.

"Did you see Evel after the day of the jump?"

Rita recalls that he did come back to Twin Falls after that a couple of times but without fanfare. Mike was still trying to smooth over some of the bad feelings that were simmering in Twin Falls.

I bring up the fact that some say he left unpaid bills, and Rita says as far as she knows bills were paid. Evel didn't leave the hotels or restaurants hanging, and Mike would have felt terrible if any of the bills coming from connections he'd made for services had been left unpaid. Destruction by the vandals was blamed on Evel, and he was being held accountable for the damage left in his wake. Insurance coverage, required by Evel and all of the vendors, provided less coverage, as it turned out, than many anticipated. But, that's another story.

"Did Mike get paid for the work he'd done?" I ask.

Rita shakes her head. "Eventually, yes, but far less than what he'd earned." She admits that Mike probably did it as much for the thrill and experience as anything, and they all ended up with stories to share.

Rita tells me that after she moved to Boise, Evel called a couple of times, once because he'd purchased a puppy for his daughter, but because of living arrangements, she was unable to keep it, and he wondered if Rita's daughter might like a puppy. Rita remembers at the time she was single, they weren't in a position for a pet either, and she wasn't sure she wanted to get together with Evel anyway. She remembered how intimidating she'd found him when they met in Twin Falls, so this encounter didn't go beyond the phone call.

Several years later, he called again and told Rita he had something he wanted to give her. Feeling a bit more secure, and also curious, she agreed to get together. She was surprised to see how much he had aged as his crippled body moved slowly around the room. It turned out he'd brought a number of pieces of his artwork to the Red Lion Riverside where he was staying on the Boise River. He told her to take whatever she wanted. She picked several, one a floral that she especially liked. He signed it, "These flowers are lovely like you, Rita." This is when Evel did make a pass. Rita let him know their friendship was "too important to complicate, and Mike's loyalty to him was unconditional." She left right away. That's the last time she saw him.

Well, there, I'm thinking, but I'm also thinking there's no indication that Evel ever forced himself on a woman. Rita let him know this wasn't going to happen, and she left without further advances from Evel.

I tell Rita that I did a little research and was unable to verify that Evel actually painted any of the pictures he was hawking and also gifting to his friends. "Do you think he painted them?"

"I'd like to think he did." She says she didn't get around to framing them, but packed them carefully when she married a wonderful guy, a dentist, and relocated to Hawaii. When the moving truck was unloaded, the paintings were nowhere to be found. She guesses they were thrown out with the wrapping and packaging materials. She feels bad that they were lost, and even recalls reading that some of them had become quite valuable, fetching a price of up to $25,000. If they were authentic Evel Knievel paintings.

I can tell that Rita has mixed feelings about the man. Charismatic. Bigger than life. Generous with friends. Yet, sometimes thoughtless and inconsiderate of others.

She leaves me with another story, a good memory. "There is a record album, an inspirational recording in Evel's own words. I remember Tim used to listen to it every night before he went to sleep when he was a boy. Evel told kids to be good. To be true to their word. To never give up." She smiles at the recollection. "Very inspirational," she muses. "He talked a good game," she says, and then, "He was a complex person."

"As we all are," I add.

JIM JONES

Jim Jones' Evel Knievel story came to me without having to go far from home or reach out to a stranger with an interview request. As Twin Falls marks the 50th anniversary of Evel's attempted Snake River Canyon jump, Jim and I celebrate 30 years of marriage.

Jim Jones was born at the old Magic Valley Memorial Hospital in Twin Falls, the same hospital where, some years later, I would enter the world. He grew up on the north side of the Snake River Canyon on a farm outside the small community of Eden. His Dad, Henry Jones, came to Idaho from Arkansas in the early 1930s, became engaged in farming, and eventually owned a large farming operation where they grew potatoes and fed cattle. Jim's mother, Eunice Martens Jones, was born in Kimberly, Idaho, one of a large family with German roots. Jim's early life was filled with aunts and uncles, and cousins, along with two sisters and a brother.

After graduating from Valley High School, Jim took off for Idaho State University in Pocatello intending to become an engineer, inspired by stories told by his Uncle Randy, who worked as a civil engineer in Afghanistan. When Jim heard President John Kennedy's 1961 inaugural address, in which Kennedy said, "Ask not what your country can do for you, but what you can do for your country," he was inspired to a public service career. He decided to be a U. S. Senator, changed his major to political science, transferred to the University of Oregon, got an ROTC commission, and went to Northwestern Law School in Chicago. A law degree and service in the military were, in Jim's eyes, necessary for a political career. After graduating from law school, he served with the U. S. Army in Vietnam, then three years as a Legislative Assistant to Idaho Senator Len Jordan in Washington D. C. After returning home to Idaho, he practiced law in Jerome (also on the north side of the Snake River Canyon,) and ran twice, without success, for the U.S. House of Representatives. In 1982, he was elected Idaho Attorney General and served eight years. Then, after fifteen years back in private practice, he was elected to the Idaho State Supreme Court, serving two terms and retiring as Chief Justice.

Though Jim and I both came from the Magic Valley, and our families were both engaged in agricultural-related businesses—Jim's dad feeding cattle, my dad owning a meat packing plant with his brothers—we didn't meet until we were both living in Boise. Jim was serving his last year as Attorney General and I was working at the Idaho State Tax Commission. We were both single parents, with three children between us, two pre-teen daughters, and a teenage son. One of the Deputy Attorneys General at the Tax Commission thought we had a lot in common with our Magic Valley roots and decided we should get together. Five years after that first set-up date, we married.

Sometime later, almost twenty years into our marriage, I started doing research to write a fictitious story to publish in 2014 for the 40th anniversary of the Evel Knievel jump. Earlier, Jim and I had talked about being in Twin Falls on the day of the jump. Anyone who'd grown up in the area and was still within driving distance was certainly curious enough about all the excitement and activity to return home to witness the event of the century scheduled to take place on Sunday afternoon, September 8, 1974. On that fateful afternoon, I was sitting with family at the Holiday Inn golf course, and Jim was at a friend's home on Falls Avenue, on the rooftop where they could get a view probably similar to mine—Evel going straight up, then straight down. Though we separately witnessed this event from different perspectives, our paths would not officially cross until fifteen years later.

Well, Jim had another story. "I represented Evel in a case," he told me casually one day as the topic of Evel Knievel and Twin Falls came up in conversation.

"What?" I hadn't heard this story before. "Like in court? You met Evel?"

"Well, no. I never actually spoke to Evel or met him."

I can't remember exactly when or where this conversation took place, certainly not in the setting of a formal interview. But, as I moved forward, with the idea of republishing my story, doing a 50th Anniversary edition of *Evel Knievel Jumps the Snake River Canyon*, I'd quiz Jim at various times . . . over morning cereal, a walk along the Boise Greenbelt. Sometimes, when we were out with friends and catching up, they'd ask if I was writing, if I was working on a new project. When I told them I was republishing my novella about Evel Knievel for the 50th anniversary of the jump, but deleting the short stories and including interviews from a select group of witnesses who were there, I'd always mentioned that Jim once represented Evel Knievel in a lawsuit. This made for interesting conversation and often filled in gaps in Jim's Evel Knievel story for me to consider.

Jim's story started several years after the jump when he got a call from Jim May, who was Evel's Twin Falls attorney. Because of the intricacies of maneuvering through various legal and logistical aspects of preparing for the jump, Evel had his own Twin Falls lawyer. He'd even established a separate corporation, Snake River Canyon Enterprises Inc. After the failed jump, lawsuits started popping up all over the place, particularly because of damage that was done, during the days before and the afternoon and evening of the jump at the launch site, as well as on city and county-owned properties. Thousands of campers had congregated at the Shoshone Falls and in Twin Falls parks and, though many were courteous and cleaned up after themselves, some were not and had left a mess. These areas just weren't set up to accommodate so many visitors, particularly those setting up campsites. This was in addition to the outright vandalism and theft on the site where the Skycycle was scheduled to launch. Depending on the source for information on crowd size, there were from 5,000 to 50,000 spectators along the canyon rim.

All of the vendors on site, as well as Evel, were required to have comprehensive public liability insurance. Evel himself was no longer insurable because of his dangerous, and some might say reckless, choice of profession. Broken bones and damaged body parts were no longer insurable and Evel had to cover these injuries himself. But he did have the required insurance for any liabilities as specifically set out in various contracts with the city, county, and BLM. The targeted landing spot on the north side of the canyon was federal property.

After the September 8, 1974 event, it seems no one felt they were responsible for the damage, and the vandals who had come into town for the excitement, leaving a trail of destruction behind, were long gone. Vendors had purchased the required insurance to hawk any number of items—generally food, such as burgers and ice cream. Beer and soda were especially popular on that hot, dry, and dusty day in early September. Well, after the failed jump, the insured vendors went to Evel, who in turn went to the insurance company, to recover losses. The insurance company refused to pay. This resulted in a number of lawsuits, with a seemingly never-ending series of claims, cross-claims, counterclaims, amended cross-claims, and amended counter-claims, eventually making its way to the Idaho Supreme Court in 1980.

Jim recalls that when Jim May first called, asking if he would represent Evel in a lawsuit, he explained he had a conflict as he had obtained the insurance policy for Evel and would be required to testify in court himself.

Jim Jones's memories of the lawsuit in which he was involved are fuzzy in some aspects, but the memory of one defendant in a lawsuit brought by Foremost Insurance Company against Evel remains vivid. In this particular case, there were a total of ten separate litigants, including Robert C. Knievel, Snake River Canyon Enterprises Inc., the Twin Falls J. C.s, and several other concessioners on site the day of the jump, including a Twin Falls resident named Antonio Guanche. Antonio was originally from the Canary Islands and spoke in a heavy French-Italian dialect.

Jim told me Antonio was selling beer, ice cream, and sandwiches. The description of one particular sandwich stands out in Jim's memory. Antonio was selling lamb burgers. Neither Jim nor I could picture the leather-clad, tough-looking motorcycle gang members, particularly the Hell's Angels, partaking of lamb burgers on the dusty edge of the canyon. The beer, on the other hand, proved to be in great demand to the point that many partakers were merely *taking* without paying.

As Jim first told me the story, I recalled the name Antonio Guanche, and remembered, in addition to serving as chef at the Blue Lakes Inn, he had opened a fancy restaurant in Twin Falls probably during the 70s. I'm guessing this was after the jump, but I'm not sure of the date. He called it Antoine's (pronounced in the French way, An-twon's), and it was one of those fancy, special occasion places. I'm not sure I ever went there, but looking back it is difficult to fathom that Twin Falls was ready for French cuisine at the time.

Jim offered to get a copy of the court transcript for the case in which he was initially involved to refresh his memory and give me the information I might need to write his story. As we waited for the requested copy of the court hearing, Jim and I engaged in additional conversations.

"So, how did you communicate with Evel?" I was confused about how an attorney could represent a client in court having never met or spoken with him.

Jim explained he did speak by phone several times to Evel's business manager in his Butte, Montana office. "Every month,

I'd send a bill," he told me. "I'd get a call from Evel's business manager and she'd confirm, "Yes, we received the bill."

"So, Evel did pay you?"

"No, never got a cent from Evel."

Throughout the time I was doing research for both my 2014 publication and the 2024 edition, I often came across articles with accusations that Evel didn't pay his bills. I'm not so sure how much of this is true. I've read several articles published many years ago, then every few years, generally as a milestone anniversary of the jump is commemorated. Most articles use the exact same words, claiming that Evel "left behind a trail of unpaid bills." This identical wording makes me wonder about the original source, if the phrase had been picked up from a single source and repeated in one article after another. Yet, I know from what Jim tells me, there were unpaid bills.

When the copy of the court transcript (dated August 1977) arrived, it proved to be an interesting piece of history. Included in *Findings of Facts:* "The defendants Knievel and Snake River Enterprises were engaged in the preparation for, and execution of, a public spectacle consisting of a motorcycle jump of the Snake River during the latter part of August, and the fore part of September, 1974." I find the word *spectacle* amusing as well as accurate.

Antonio's testimony is as colorful as Jim remembers, though as he reviewed the transcript, he reflected that, "You had to be there to get the true flavor." Yet, as I read, I find descriptions that could provide the script for a movie. Antonio explained that he came in as a last-minute vendor. A company from California was originally contracted for concessions at the jump but pulled out shortly before because they couldn't find rooms for their employees to stay in Twin Falls. The event had garnered so much attention and interest that the hotels and motels were pre-booked and 100% full.

Shortly before the scheduled jump, Antonio, who was the chef at the Blue Lakes Inn, was contacted by a Mr. Joe Vechio (sometimes spelled in the transcript as Veccio, though I'm guessing the actual spelling might be Vecchio). Vechio identified himself as an agent for Knievel Enterprises and asked Antonio if he could be a food vendor on site. Antonio was told he'd be required to have insurance, and that he could acquire it through Foremost Insurance Company, which he did, delivering a $300 check to a Mr. Cardell W. Smith, representative and agent of the insurance company. Antonio asked several times if this was full coverage and was told yes, it was.

A couple of years later, as a witness in the case, Antonio testified that, "I don't speak very English good, now, two years ago was worse, I told Joe Vechio, I speak Italian, he speak Italian, I say, 'you're sure everything is taken care of?' he said, 'it's fine, everything is taken care of.'" Antonio was borrowing equipment because of the expected demand for food and drinks and wanted to make sure he was fully covered. I can only imagine this conversation between Antonio Guanche and Joe Vechio, and I'm casting the parts in a movie in my head as I read the court transcript.

During his testimony, Antonio described how the beer was looted, but he doesn't recall specifically if this was Friday or Saturday night. He was still working every day at the Blue Lakes Inn, but he was back and forth between the two locations over the weekend. "I was working two places," he said.

He also explained how Evel was involved. "Evel Knievel, he gave the notice to give it for one hour for free and he'd take care of the tab." But the crowd was not content with one free beer, and according to Antonio, within ten minutes, the beer was gone. "They jump inside the concession and take the cases." He estimated over the weekend, they took 2,000 cases of beer. He goes on to describe the crowd. "They all have long hairs and beards, big knives on them, saying, 'Peace brother,' and all I was saying, 'Peace, brother—' " He admits he was scared.

Antonio was also selling fruit. "They play football with these. I see cantaloupes and watermelons everywhere."

Jim describes Antonio's testimony as animated, amplified by facial expressions and gestures. He often had the courtroom, including the judge, in stitches.

Then, the meat for the lamb burgers . . . vandals broke into the truck where the meat was stored, destroying thousands of pounds, tossing meat on the floor, dust and gravel flying everywhere. "I have $10,000, $12,000 worth of meat, roasts, whole lambs, roast beef I buy from Zweigart Company, everything was on credit . . ." Antonio testified. He described the mob climbing onto the top of the truck and smashing a hole through the roof. They also destroyed a custom-made metal grill. "I have a big grill, three by five," he said. ". . . they saw it in pieces . . ." Sunday night, after the failed jump, any equipment that remained was torched. "I went to see," Antonio continued, "everything was on fire, I see the fire there you know, . . . very expensive equipment, equipment I borrow from Meadow Gold, equipment I buy, I have all these bills, warmers, freezers and everything was burned."

As I read the transcript of the case, particularly Antonio's testimony, my initial amusement was overcome by horror and sympathy. I was seeing some injustice here, especially when I read the explanation for why the insurance company was not required to pay the policyholders for losses. The court document quotes an exclusion in the policy: "It is agreed the insurance does not apply to bodily injury or property damage arising out of riot, civil commotion or out of mob action . . ." Judge Cunningham— who just happened to be my neighbor and lived on Tenth Avenue just a few houses down and across the alley from where I grew up—ruled that there was a riot, which relieved Foremost from liability for the concessioners' damage.

I learned from Jim, that, as the remaining lawsuits against Evel worked through the court system, Judge Cunningham determined that, because Antonio was never given a copy of the insurance policy and he believed from what he had been told, that the policy provided full coverage, the insurance company

162

must cover his loses. I don't know how the other defendants fared.

I also learned that, although Evel never paid the legal bills Jim continued to send to Butte until the case was fully settled, he was paid by Foremost Insurance Company because the court required it to pay "a reasonable attorney fee" for defending Knievel and Snake River Canyon Enterprises, Inc. Jim's payment came after the lawsuit was heard by the Idaho Supreme Court in 1980, six years after Evel's attempted jump, three years after Jim became involved.

I'm happy and feel some satisfaction knowing that Antonio Guanche, the enterprising, hard-working, forward-thinking chef and business entrepreneur, who aspired to sell French food in Twin Falls and lamb burgers to Hell's Angels, eventually recovered his losses.

Maybe after 50 years and substantial growth, Twin Falls is now ready for fancy French cuisine; I'm still skeptical about those lamb burgers for Hell's Angels.

SUE SWENSON CUMMINS

Sue Swenson Cummins and I graduated in the same class at Twin Falls High School but didn't get acquainted until years later in Boise. A group of Twin Falls class of '66 girls (many grandmas and even great-grandmas now!) living in the Boise area have gathered for the past few years for a monthly lunch, and it was through one of these lunches that I learned Sue had an Evel Knievel story, too.

We were sitting across the table at Ling & Louie's in Meridian visiting when Sue said she'd heard I wrote a book about Evel Knievel and told me she had helped out with the parking on the Qualls' Ranch the day of the jump. Knowing there was a crowd of anywhere from 5,000 to 50,000—depending on the source—I could only imagine what a mess an unpaved, unmarked parking lot on a dusty pasture might create. I was curious. When Sue said she was directing traffic on horseback I knew I wanted to learn more. The image of an Idaho cowgirl on a horse, herding not sheep or cattle but Hell's Angels, was forming in my mind and I definitely wanted to talk to her about her memories of the jump. Sue also had stories from her late dad, O. K. Swenson, who supplied portable toilets for the spectators. The name was familiar to me as I had seen it on legal documents and knew that Mr. Swenson was among the numerous vendors and service providers hoping to collect from Foremost Insurance Company and, of course, from Evel himself, for their destroyed property.

I told Sue about my plan to republish the book in 2024 to commemorate the attempted jump and shared that I was gathering stories from people who were there to include in this second edition. We exchanged numbers, both of us eager to get together. Over the next couple of weeks, we made and canceled a couple of coffee dates. I got knocked down by a bout of Covid, surprised that I had managed to dodge it for the past three years, and so I had to lay low for a couple of weeks. By the time we finally got together for lunch in Boise, I had a shorter window of opportunity to meet in person as Sue and her husband Terry were leaving soon to winter in Arizona.

Finally, we join up for lunch. I'm interested in knowing more about Sue and her family, particularly because we graduated the same year, yet never had any classes together and didn't know each other back then. Conversation comes easily and we laugh about the fact that we have no memories of one another. She was born in Wyoming and spent much of her early childhood in North Dakota where her dad had a furniture store. The family moved to Twin Falls when she was in grade school.

"How did you end up in Twin Falls?" I ask, always curious why someone who wasn't born in Twin Falls would end up in a small community in south-central Idaho.

"I think my dad had passed through on a business trip and liked the town, liked the idea of milder winters."

"Twin Falls has plenty of snow in the winter." I think of the snow that was normal back when we were kids, though as a child that was certainly not a problem. Building snowmen, creating snow angels in the yard, and even wrapping up in our winter wool and plodding through several feet of snow on our way to school are all good childhood memories.

"We were coming from North Dakota," Sue explains.

"Oh, yeah." I realize those North Dakota winters could be harsh, temperatures often dropping well below zero for extended periods.

166

"What did your dad do in Twin Falls?"

"He opened another furniture store, Swenson Furniture down on Main." I have only a vague memory of this, never having been in a position to buy furniture in Twin Falls. Sue tells me she has an older sister Judy who was several years ahead of us in school. "Dad bought some property in the canyon, about halfway down the Shoshone Falls grade, to build a home."

Sue attended several grade schools, and by the time she was in junior high, the family was living in the canyon where they built their new home. She describes the sizable property—big enough to keep horses, though it wasn't farmland—as being located just before the pay booth to enter the Shoshone Falls Park. The house was situated on a ledge with a great view of the falls. When the flow of the waterfalls was at its peak, they could feel the mist while sitting on their porch. Like many of those I have interviewed, Sue's connection to the Snake River Canyon began much before Evel Knievel came to town.

"How did you get to school?" I ask.

"We walked up the grade, then caught the bus, until Dad bought me a car, a '39 Chevy!"

"A '39 Chevy?" We both laugh. This would have been an old car back in the sixties when we were in high school, and I can't even begin to picture a '39 Chevy now.

Sue married about a year after graduating, a boy from Murtaugh, a nearby farming community. Sue's husband, Terry, worked in agriculture-related businesses, at Cummins Farms with his father and brothers, and then eventually started his own business, selling seed. Sue and Terry raised two daughters, Ginger and Shani, in Eden and Murtaugh. She worked in Twin Falls, first as a secretary for two different lawyers, in the mornings for Harry Turner, and in the afternoons for Golden Bennett. From there she went on to the Twin Falls Police Department, typing police reports, search warrants, and criminal complaints. When a position came up as a city detective, Sue applied and got the job. From the Twin Falls Police Department,

167

she went on to the Idaho Department of Correction where she worked as a probation and parole officer for several years. I'm especially curious about her duties as a police detective and I'm tempted to veer off in that direction but pull myself back to the original intention of our getting together—Evel Knievel. I wonder if Sue's involvement was through her work at the Twin Falls Police Department, which was where she would have been in '74. I know there was concern all over town with the influx of questionable Evel Knievel fans, and law enforcement officials were on alert, though Evel supposedly hired his own security.

When I ask about this, Sue tells me there was plenty of chatter around the office in the months leading up to Evel's jump. At the time, the Chief of Police was Frank Barnett. Tim Qualls, who had leased the canyon rim property to Evel, was Chief of Detectives. Sue remembers the jump was on a Sunday afternoon, so it would have been outside her regular working hours. She and several others from the police department got involved in the parking control through Tim Qualls. Her husband, Terry, was also on site, helping to direct traffic, not on horseback, like Sue, but on a motorcycle.

"Did you meet Evel?"

"Yes, I think it was the week before the jump out at the Qualls' place, at a meeting as we were getting ready for the event."

"Did you have a preconceived notion of Evel?"

"I was aware of who he was before he came to Twin Falls. I knew he was a daredevil, crazy, that he'd broken a lot of bones performing his stunts. But, I didn't have any particular negative feelings."

"What was your impression when you met him in person?"

"Suave, big ego," she replies without giving it much thought.

"How about the days before the jump? Were you seeing the strangers coming into town? Were you apprehensive or worried that this could be a dangerous time?"

"I worked in Twin, but lived in Eden, so I just came in for

168

work, then back home. So no, I didn't really see that before the jump."

"Tell me about the day of the jump."

"We dropped the girls off at Mom and Dad's. They were living in town by then. My sister Judy and her husband had moved into the house in the canyon. We hauled the horse out to the Qualls' place in a trailer."

"What was it like at the Qualls' Ranch that day as the crowds gathered?"

"The number of people was overwhelming. I don't think the promoters or anyone was ready for that."

Sue describes some of what she saw. "I remember a group of guys getting out of a motor home and tossing around a frisbee." Maybe not so unusual, but Sue then tells me they were all nude, so probably not what we were used to seeing on a Sunday afternoon. "A couple of guys came by and asked me if my horse was grazing on grass. One of them pulled out a plastic baggie filled with marijuana and even offered to feed some to my horse."

"Were you shocked? Surprised at what you saw?" I knew Sue had probably been exposed to more than I could fathom seeing in Twin Falls back then because of her work in the police department, especially as a detective, but even so—naked hippies, motorcycle gangs with weed!

"The thing that surprised me," Sue replies, "was the families coming in with kids. This was not a nice environment." Sue shakes her head and I'm sure, at the time, she was thinking of her own children, then four and six, safe with Grandma and Grandpa.

"Were you afraid?"

Sue says she wasn't afraid, but she admits to being disappointed when they got called back from the area sectioned off for parking. It was a good distance from the ramp, and by the time Evel launched his Skycycle, they were back at the Qualls' house sitting on a corral fence and not well-positioned to witness the jump itself. They did see the rocket go up, and then quickly down. It was evident that Evel didn't make it to the other side of the canyon, but they had no idea until later what had happened to him. She remembers seeing smoke, and later, fires burning near the launch site.

The mention of fires makes me think of the portable toilets that I know were supplied by Sue's dad, O. K. Swenson.

"Your dad had provided the chemical toilets on site. What can you tell me about that? How did your dad get involved?"

Sue says that her dad was an entrepreneur, finding any possible opportunity to turn a profit. Besides owning the furniture store, he invested in real estate and purchased military surplus vehicles to fix up and resale.

I know many in Twin Falls made money because of the event: the motels, restaurants, gas stations, and grocery stores. But the belief that Evel left a trail of unpaid bills still lingers. Most of that, I believe, has to do with damage by the unruly crowds after the failed launch.

I've brought along a folder with copies of news articles—those portable toilets were making headlines even before the jump. One story with the headline "Toilet problem," was printed five days before the jump, and Mr. Swenson was already considering what he would do with 200 chemical toilets after the jump. It seems he had numerous possibilities, including leasing them to a Jackpot, Nevada, casino to use on their golf course, or to building sites and for large outdoor gatherings, which were now required by federal law to supply sanitary facilities. As it turned out, this wasn't a decision he would have to make. The outdoor toilets were trashed, burned, and toppled by the rowdy mob after Evil failed to perform to their expectations. Because of the number of toilets needed, O. K. Swenson had to build, as well as purchase, the toilets. Many were constructed of wood, and thus easily set on fire. Stories are told of gang members on motorcycles jumping over the flaming remains. The saga of the toilet problem would continue for years as the various lawsuits to recover losses made their way through the court systems in both Idaho and Montana.

Sue says she wasn't directly involved in the leasing of the toilets, but the information in the articles seems to be mostly accurate, though she was surprised at the number of toilets. Swenson was paid $19,000 upfront to lease the 200 chemical toilets. The original contract was for $25,000, and he was suing Evel for the $6,000 still due, as well as attorney fees, court costs, and interest. As we flip through the various news articles, I point out the frequent mention of O. K. Swenson. According to an article published in August 1977, the court ruled that the insurance company would not be required to cover any of the damage because of the riot clause in the policy. In October 1979, a judgment was issued in Swenson's favor and Evel, who failed to appear in court, was ordered to pay $9,700. Sue remembers that the lawsuits went on for years, even after her dad, angry and intent on pursuing Evel, passed away. In a press release put out by the Associated Press in 2002, it was reported that Sue's mother, Esther (Toni), the surviving spouse, filed documents in July of that year, asking the Butte District Court to enforce the judgment from 1979, which had still not been collected. Sue's former employer, attorney Harry Turner, represented the family. Harry was a well-respected attorney in town, known for his legal skills as well as his adventurous spirit. Sue says that he enjoyed both water and snow skiing, especially remarkable because Harry was blind.

"Your dad didn't live to collect what was owed him? How about your mom and family, were you finally able to collect on this?"

Sue tells me no, they were not. She remembers an ill-fated attempt to collect in 1999. For the 25th anniversary of the jump, Evel Knievel came back to Twin Falls, appearing at various venues, including the Magic Valley Mall where Skycycle X2 was on display. In a *Times-News* article about the 25th anniversary, Evel is described as a sixty-year-old "stooped, chalk-haired motorcyclist." Knievel had resumed performing his stunts following the colossal failure of the Twin Falls jump, and his physical condition continued to deteriorate. His life as a daredevil and stuntman had taken its toll.

Even after twenty years, the judgment from 1979 against Evel had still not been paid and Harry Turner saw Evel's return to Twin Falls as a perfect opportunity to send the sheriff out to serve a writ of execution. Because of his difficulty with mobility, Evel was moving around the mall in a golf cart. When he was served, he flew into a rage and angrily flung the papers onto the floor. Sue said that she and her sister Judy think Harry Turner should have just attached the rocket and sold it to settle the debt.

Sue recalls that she and Judy were interviewed at some time during the lengthy stretch of legal battles that continued even after her dad died. A reporter and photographer from a newspaper in Las Vegas met them at Harry Turner's Blue Lakes home in Twin Falls. She remembers few details about the interview itself, though the reporter confessed he'd come prepared to interview a couple of Idaho crackpots. He said he found Sue and Judy much different than expected, that he found them credible. "He was basically saying this was not a frivolous lawsuit, that we were above board, that we were okay," Sue says.

I wonder if the reporter initially thought, perhaps like Evel when he first came to town, that Twin Falls was home to a bunch of hicks and suckers. Who else would believe that a daredevil like Evel Knievel could jump the Snake River Canyon on a motorcycle that wasn't even a motorcycle, and even encourage him with their involvement? I do wonder how many believed he would make it to the other side. Yet, many were willing to let him give it a try.

Sue doesn't seem particularly upset by the events of 50 years ago or even by the fact that her dad never fully collected on the debt. Others are still upset, convinced of Evel's evil intentions. Yet, he brought to Twin Falls a certain recognition, which some might describe as notoriety. Good or bad, this is debatable. But,

Evel put the town, and especially the Snake River Canyon, on the map.

My mom and dad used to volunteer at the original Twin Falls Visitor Center, a small 600-square-foot building on the canyon rim, which was replaced by the present, modern, and much larger center in 2014. Dad once told me the second most frequently asked question was, "Where did Evel Knievel jump the canyon?"

Of course, I was curious, and I'd asked, "What's the first most asked question?"

"Where are the toilets?" my dad replied with a grin.

As I think of my dad's story, I have to acknowledge that Sue's dad, O. K. Swenson, was certainly aware that if thousands of people were to visit Twin Falls to see Evel Knievel jump the Snake River Canyon, one of the first things needed to welcome them to the city was toilets. Needless to say, it would have turned out better for all, Evel included, if these guests had behaved themselves.

Thank you for reading *Evel Knievel Jumps the Snake River Canyon*. If you enjoyed the story, please post a review on Amazon.com or Goodreads.com

You might also enjoy Kelly's other books:

Angel Boy

Bloodline and Wine

Lost and Found in Prague

The Woman Who Heard Color

The Lost Madonna

The Seventh Unicorn

Learn more at kellyjonesbooks.com

Kelly Jones is an Idaho native. She was born and grew up in Twin Falls. She graduated from Gonzaga University in Spokane, Washington, and now lives in Boise.

Kelly can be contacted at kellyjonesbooks@gmail.com or kelly@kellyjonesbooks.com

www.ingramcontent.com/pod-product-compliance
Lightning Source LLC
Chambersburg PA
CBHW050738250626
47155CB00005B/1819